THE MULLIGAN

EDDIE LAY

EDDIE LAY

THE MULLIGAN

By

Eddie Lay

THE MULLIGAN

AUTHORS NOTES

Thank you to my wife for being the first to read and suggest changes. The original version had two endings and although I preferred the second one, I wasn't sure. After seeking help from my wife Sandy and her Aunt Sissy, both picked the first one, so I combined the two.

Granddaughters Brittany and Samantha of BS Photography in Mooresville, Indiana did a great job photographing the cover. Thank you to my daughter Michelle, granddaughter Hannah, son Mark, and my wife Sandy for making the video ad. My entire family is supportive and helpful.

COVER PHOTO: BS PHOTOGRAPHY- MOORSEVILLE, INDIANA

Join my readers club and receive a

FREE

eBook of mine

Drop me a line and request your free book. I would also love to hear what you thought about The Mulligan.

mailto:elaywriter4ebook@gmail.com?subject=Free Book

Friend me on Face Book:

www.facebook.com/eddielayebookauthor

THE MULLIGAN

THE MULLIGAN

Seven forty-five am Joe Parrish, pulls to the curb in front of Franklin Elementary. Eight-year-old Samantha grabs her back-pack and climbs out. "Bye daddy."

"Goodbye pumpkin. Have a nice day."

Every day the same thing. He drops his daughter at the curb and watches until she enters school. Every day he gets the same feeling of loss because his beautiful little girl looks so much like her late mother. Every day the same; except today.

EDDIE LAY

Twenty-two minutes after leaving his daughter's school, Joe enters Dunkin' Donuts for his morning coffee. This morning he decides to get a doughnut, but has trouble choosing one.

After several minutes he settles on a Blueberry Cake. The indecision put him four minutes and twenty-two seconds behind schedule.

For a normal person this would not be a problem, but Joe is not normal. He has to have everything neat, and in its place, and he is never late. In order to make up for the discrepancy in time Joe calculates he will have to drive four miles per hour over the speed limit.

If he had not taken the extra time to buy the donuts and if he had not been going over the speed limit, he would not have been at that intersection when another late driver failed to stop. As it was Joe did not see the Buick grill smash into his door, snapping his head sharply to the side and breaking his neck.

***

THE MULLIGAN

Joe opens his eyes and looks around. He is lying down in the middle of nothing. There is no ceiling or floor, no sky or ground. It is as if he is in a room painted all white, except there are no walls and no furniture.

SWOOSH!

"What was that?"

SWOOSH!

Something flies past his head.

Standing a few yards in front of him is a man dressed all in white and swinging a golf club.

"Hey! Watch it," Joe shouts.

The man says nothing.

"Hey. "

Jumping to his feet Joe stomps to where the man is taking a practice swing. There is a golf tee at his feet, but there isn't a ball sitting on top of it.

"I always did have trouble with my slice, you'd think that after a century or two I'd get better," the man said as he moved around for a better angle.

SWOOSH!

7

"You need to watch where you aim that thing, you almost hit me."

The man ignores Joe.

"You're not going to get any better because you don't have a ball."

"You don't need one here."

"How can you play golf without a ball...Where is here?"

SWOOSH!

"I ask where I am," Joe shouts.

The man raises his head and glares at this annoying intruder.

"You're not going to shut up, are you?"

"I need to know what direction? I can't just walk; I need to know in which direction to go."

The man uses his club to point to his right. "That way."

Joe stares where the golf club is pointing. "There's nothing in that direction."

"OK go the other way then."

"There's nothing there either."

"It doesn't matter which way you go; you'll get there."

"You're crazy!"

"I've been told that many times."

"How far is this...check-in?"

The man, concentrating on his shot, mumbles.

Joe repeats himself. "How far do I have to walk?"

The golfer glances up. "Start walking and don't stop until you get there."

Stomping off, Joe shouts over his shoulder. "Thanks for the help."

2

Disgusted, but happy to get away from this obnoxious person Joe glares into the whiteness as he heads off. Walking forward squinting his eyes as he searches all around him trying to see something, anything, but as far as he can tell there's nothing but white.

SWOOSH!

Joe turns and glares at the crazy man as something zips past his right ear.

The grinning golfer shouts, "FORE!"

THE MULLIGAN

Wondering if everyone in this place is mad Joe continues walking, but he doesn't walk long before he finds someone sitting at a table flipping the pages of a large book. The sitting man is dressed in white like the repulsive golfer. His shoulder length white hair is well groomed, but because he is seated Joe cannot tell his height, and his averted eyes hide their color.

"I suppose this is were I check-in."

Continuing to scrutinize his book, the man answers without looking up.

"You would be Joe Parrish."

"That's right, and you would be?"

"Call me Pete."

"Pete? As in Peter?"

"Yes."

"I don't suppose you would be Saint Peter, would you?"

Peter continues scanning the book.

"I prefer Pete or Peter. We're all the same here, except One."

"Right! So, you are Saint Peter, everyone is wearing white, but I don't see anyone wearing wings."

Saint Peter makes a "humph" sound and continues his reading.

Joe pinches himself. "Ouch! OK! When am I going to wake up Pete?"

St. Peter raises his head. Ebony eyes fall on Joe that seem to wrap around him with a cloak of love and serenity.

"Do you know about fifty percent of souls that arrive here think they are dreaming? You are not sleeping Joe, this is real."

"You're saying that I'm dead?"

"Pretty much."

"If that's true how did I die? I don't think I was sick, and I don't remember crashing my car."

"How about that young grad student, do you remember her?"

"Vicky? What does she have to do with it?"

"Come on! Did you really think that a fifty something law professor could keep up with a twenty something college student?"

For a moment Joe is speechless.

THE MULLIGAN

"A heart attack?"

St. Peter smiles, "Just a little Heavenly humor. You were hit by a man running a red light."

"This really isn't a dream, is it?"

St. Peter shakes his head.

While pacing back and forth in front of the table Joe talks more to himself than the man seated in front of him.

"This can't be right, I'm not dead. I can't be dead. I've got too much to get done. I'm getting ready to publish again, I'm receiving my fourth doctorate, and I'm getting tenure.

"Everything I wanted to achieve is about to transpire." A vision of a young girl flashes through Joe's mind. "Samantha! She's all alone now."

"That's no longer your concern."

"What are you talking about? She's my little girl."

"In the first place she's no longer a little girl, and the second place there's nothing you can do for her. That time is gone. Look at it this way, you have achieved social success."

Joe stops pacing and faces the man at the table.

"What do you mean, I have achieved social success?"

"Social success means you have been recognized by your peers."

"I know what it means, I meant what do you mean by saying that? Never mind, it doesn't matter. I have a beautiful eight-year-old daughter that needs me. I am all she has. I can't die now, what will happen to her?"

"She's in good hands."

"What are you talking about? Her mother died when she was six, and now me. She has no one else."

"Yes, she does, she has her aunt Gertrude."

Joe is stunned, he doesn't know any aunt named Gertrude, in fact neither he or Connie had a sister. He doesn't know anyone named Gertrude, and then it hits him, he does know a Gertrude. It can't be her, she is not Samantha's aunt. But she is the only Gertrude he knows.

"Do you mean Gertrude Brukman?"

Saint Peter nods.

"Yes. She is a wonderful woman."

"Gertrude is immature and seditious. She doesn't know how to raise a child; she is a child."

St. Peter returns his gaze to the book and thumbs through it. He stops and reads several words before replying.

"Your daughter is going to do just fine. Gertrude is doing a good job of taking care of her."

"Fine isn't good enough. Samantha is on her way to becoming a great pianist. She has the talent and ambition to be a virtuoso, but she needs me there to guide her.

"Gertrude can't guide her own hand to her butt. She doesn't know anything about music, and the only thing she can do is cause trouble. Look in your book and tell me something. Does my daughter make it to Carnegie Hall?"

St. Peter looks further back in his book.

"Not exactly."

"OK, but she is on her way, isn't she?"

"No."

"You see? I told you Gertie doesn't know how to lead a young girl in the right direction."

"Gertrude had nothing to do with it. Samantha quit playing after your death."

Joe's volume of speech goes up.

"She can't quit, it would be asinine to waste all of her talent. This is what I'm talking about. Neither her mother nor I would have permitted her to quit playing the piano. Gertie doesn't know how to mold her into the woman she can be.

Samantha has a gift just as her mother did, and when you hear the music that comes out you can tell she loves to play. I can't let her throw all that talent away. I have to go back."

Joe turns and starts walking back the way he came.

St. Peter leans back in his chair with his hands up.

"You can't go back Joe."

Stubbornly Joe continues walking as he calls back over his shoulder.

"Watch me."

After he takes three more steps Joe finds himself back in front of St. Peter. Stopping short he looks to either side and then turns left. Three more steps and he is facing St. Peter again. He turns right but it is a futile move.

Joe's face flushes and he is practically screaming.

"Stop that! I'm going back! Somehow, someway I am going back."

"Joe, you have to resign yourself to the fact that you can no longer influence what happens to Samantha, and what does happen is for the best."

Joe's head falls to his chest and his shoulders slouch.

"Do you know what would happen to her if I didn't die?"

"No, I don't."

"So how do you know this is for the best?"

"Because this has been written by much greater power than me. HE knows all that could be and all that will be."

"That may be but I need to know for myself."

Joe's voice becomes softer, his face saddens, and his eyes are pleading.

"I have to be sure my little girl becomes the best she can be. Isn't there some way I could go back? Just until I'm convinced this is the best for her?"

A lot of souls stand in front of St. Peter's desk every day, so he is accustomed to their frantic request to return to their old lives.

"Of the fifty percent who accept what has happened to them half want to return. I'm sorry, but you can't go back. It has been written that you die on the twenty fourth of..."

St. Peter rapidly sifts through the book once more. He pauses and looks at Joe, and then stands up and walks over to where a man in a gold robe appears; they talk. The body movements and flailing arms indicate that the discussion is a heated one. From the expression on St. Peter's face as he returns, Joe concludes that something is definitely wrong.

"Your life has been exemplary, except for a few slip-ups, or maybe more than a few the last years of your life. Your love for your wife and your dedication to teaching is admirable. To permit you to return however, is not within my power to grant. I will have to go to a higher authority."

"And – – –?"

"And?"

"Will you do it?"

"I'll try."

"GREAT!"

"Don't get too excited. The chances of it happening are not very good. Permitting a soul to return to the mortal world rarely happens."

"But it has happened hasn't it? "

"Yes, it has."

"So, you will try, won't you?"

"I'll do my best, but it is complicated to do. There are a thousand details that have to be in order. Forget just one of them and, well, it's better if you don't. However, since it was our fault, I'll see what I can do."

"That's all I ask."

St. Peter disappears and Joe says, "THANK YOU."

No sooner do the words escape Joe's lips and St. Peter is back.

"Sorry it took so long, but this is a big decision that can have enormous repercussions. It can change a timeline that will affect more than you can imagine. Just one wrong word or an angry outburst by you can change the destiny of millions of people. By doing or not doing something can ---"

"OK, okay, so… "

St. Peter says nothing.

Joe's patience is wearing thin.

"What did you decide? Tell me, can I go back?"

St. Peter appears a little embarrassed.

"As I said before there has been a bit of a mix-up. You were supposed to come up here on the twenty fourth, but it is the twenty fourth of next month."

"Are you saying that I died a month too soon?"

"These are trying times and our collectors are a little over worked right now. Mistakes do happen."

"No! No! Angels don't make mistakes."

Peter continues not looking at Joe.

"Collectors are not angels, and all of us do make mistakes. Only God doesn't make mistakes. Now we have to correct this mistake."

"Does that mean I get to go back?"

"Yes – – – "

Joe let's out a sigh.

"Thank you."

Peter turns to face Joe, his eyes soft with empathy.

"– – – but with restrictions."

"What kind restrictions?"

"You can't do anything that will drastically change the future."

"How am I going to know what that is?"

"A guide will accompany you to prevent you from doing something you shouldn't."

"Is that all?"

St. Peter steps around the table in front of Joe.

"No! You cannot tell your daughter you are her father."

"That's not fair, anyway when she sees me, she will know who I am."

"No, she won't."

"She won't? Why not?"

"You'll appear to her as a completely different person."

"Why? What's wrong with going back as myself?"

"There are numerous reasons, too many to go into, just take my word for it."

"Who will she think I am?"

"That hasn't been decided yet."

"When do you intend to decide?"

"Returning a soul to Earth is a little tricky. We can't just plop it anywhere. There has to be a vessel available to house it."

"A what? Never mind, just find one, and fast."

"Did you ever hear the old adage 'Patience is a virtue'?"

Joe waves his hand as a signal to stop talking.

"Are there any other… restrictions?"

"You will have one month, your time, then you will have to return here."

"Only a month?"

"You have to return the day that is written."

"I thought I would get to see my little girl grow up."

"I'm afraid not. If you don't accept these conditions, we will have to forget the whole thing."

"Don't do that! I'll make this work, some way. When do I go?"

"First you will meet your guide, and you will have to wait for the right body."

"What are you talking about, the right body, why can't I use mine? I like my body. I am comfortable with it." Joe holds his hands up. "You can change the way I look. Make me taller, or heavier. You can even make me Asian, or Indian, or any nationality you want, just let me keep my body."

THE MULLIGAN

"I am afraid that yours won't do. It has been too long since your death. You need a new one, and you have to step into that body the second it is vacated for this to work."

"What do you mean too long? I've only been here a few minutes."

"I'm afraid not. Your body has deteriorated too much for us to be able to use it."

"Deteriorated? That takes a long time, doesn't it? How long has it been?"

"Time in our realm and the human realm is different. Time here goes much slower than there."

"How much slower?"

"Your eight-year-old daughter is now a senior in high school."

"She's a senior? I missed 10 years of her life?"

"I'm afraid so."

Joe slumps to whatever it is they use for a floor.

St. Peter studies the man in front of him sitting with his hands in his lap and head bowed. The sight dredges up more sympathy from the keeper of the Golden Gates.

"You CAN see everything in her life that you missed if you want."

Joe doesn't move.

"We can sort of put everything on rewind and you can view it; much like instant replay."

Joe raises his tear-streaked face.

"It's not like being there, but…" St. Peter shrugs.

A weak smile spreads across Joe's face. St. Peter helps him stand and as they walk off St. Peter puts his arm around Joe's shoulder and asks:

"Would you like butter on your popcorn?"

THE MULLIGAN

3

After watching is little girl grow up in an instant right before his eyes Joe is alone in the white void as he marvels at the thought that it is like watching home movies. St. Peter is right; it isn't the same as being there, but he is grateful that he got to see everything he missed. Now he is anxious to see her again. She isn't the sweet little girl that he knows, so he will have to get to know this young woman she is now.

A familiar voice comes from behind him; it is that crazy golfer again. Joe thought he was rid of his annoying belligerent attitude. "How did you swing this?"

"What?"

When Joe turns around, he and the crazy golfer are standing face to face.

23

"They granted you a Mulligan; no one ever gets a mulligan around here, how did you talk them into it?"

"A Mulligan? What is a Mulligan?"

"It's a golfing term; a Mulligan is a do-over. It's a second chance to do something right."

"I know you love to hit a little white ball around, but were you a professional golfer or something?"

"Yes, I was. I toured the world playing in tournaments. I made and spent a million dollars."

"You have got to be kidding. You made a million dollars by knocking a little ball into a hole."

"And I did it all without a college degree."

Aggravated that the crazy person has returned, Joe turns and walks away trying to put distance between the two. However, his tormentor follows, close on his heels.

Joe shouts over his shoulder, "Isn't there a golf game or torture session you have to get to?"

"No, I have nothing pressing at the moment. Tell me how you did it. How did you get a Mulligan? You have something on Peter, don't you? I'll bet it is something juicy. Tell me what it is, I promise not to tell."

"What is the matter with you? Are you insane? I don't have anything on anyone."

"It's just that as long as I've been here, and that is quite a while, I have never seen anyone go back. Plenty have begged, and screamed, and threw tantrums, but no one has ever returned to the human world."

Joe continues walking but he picks up the pace in an effort to escape this irritating man.

"Do you annoy everyone that shows up here?"

"Not everyone. Most of the souls that arrive are ecstatic to be here. But the ones that aren't are either in denial and think they are dreaming, or they think they are too young to die. There's something different about you; I don't know what it is but I like you."

"Lucky me."

"Come on now, fess up. How did you pull it off? If you don't have some juicy tid-bit on Pete, then you must have mighty strong connections"

Joe resigns himself to the fact that he is not going to be rid of this annoyance until he leaves this place and returns to Earth.

"It seems they screwed up and I died too soon. They brought me up here a month before it was time, so Peter agreed to let me go back for the time that I missed; he seems to be fair."

"He's a pushover. His compassion gets in the way of making a rational decision sometimes."

"What do you mean?"

"There are souls here that should not be."
Joe stops.
"I don't believe that."
"Oh, you don't do you?"
Anger seeps into Joe's voice. He confronts his adversary face to face.
"No! I don't."
"You've not been here long enough to make that observation."
"If he wasn't doing the job right, I think he would have been replaced by now. I don't have time to listen to your negative attitude, why don't you go to a corner somewhere and play with your invisible golf balls, and putt around until you find someone else to aggravate?"
"Ha, ha! You're more fun than a whoopee cushion. By the time we get back you and I will be best friends."
"Get back from where? You're not – – –?"
"FORE!"

4

Joe and the golfer are standing in front of a large golden gate. There's nothing else in sight, just Joe, the golfer, and the gate.

"Before we go back, there are a few rules you have to know about and abide by. Number one is that you cannot tell your daughter who you really are. You're going to want to so bad you think you're going to burst, but DON'T DO IT!"

"I know, I will be in someone else's body so I'll look like someone else to her. St. Peter told me, but how will it hurt to tell her who I am? She has a right to know."

"No, she doesn't. First of all, she will not believe you, and second it is one of the rules, in fact it is the number one rule. Number two rule; if I tell you not to interfere with something that is happening, listen to me.

"You can't fix everything in her life and some things that seem to be bad will eventually be for the best. So, if I say let it go, let it go."

"You are one bad-ass, aren't you? What is your name?"

"Walter Hagan, but my friends call me The Haig."

"What kind of name is that? The Haig! Did you say Haig are hag? There's no way I'm going to call you 'The Haig'."

"Be careful, you do not want to get me angry. Did you hear me say friends call me that?"

"I didn't think Angels got angry. What about turning the other cheek?"

"I'm not an angel, I'm a guide and we do a lot of things that you would not like."

"I'm S-o-r-r-y!"

"You should be. This isn't a joke, or a game. Lives of other people than you or your daughters are at stake. You may think what you are changing is for the good, but it could turn out for worse. Stopping someone from dying could be a mistake, because, they might become a serial killer later. Do you understand?"

"I suppose."

"Come on, a body has been found for you."

"It's about time. It's been what… ten minutes? Who am I going to be? A handsome movie star, CEO of a Fortune five hundred company, or... I know... the president of the United States."

"Or a pet snake!"

Joe gasps.

"You're kidding." Under his breath, "I hope."

5

Joe wakes up again in an all-white room. This one however does have walls and a ceiling. He is lying down staring up at a ceiling with swirls, and a fan slowly turning over his head. Cool air swirls around him bringing in the smell of jasmine through an open window.

Turning his head to the right he sees the window partially covered with bamboo curtains and a view of a small yard surrounded by a privacy fence. What little grass there is, is well manicured. A table with a lamp and phone sitting on it is under the window. The lamp is a modernistic thing made of chrome, and very ugly.

THE MULLIGAN

He realizes that he is lying in a bed and by looking past his feet at the opposite wall he sees what appears to be an antique dresser with a door beside it.

The door is partially open revealing a bathroom that has pale green walls. Haig is standing by his bed wearing a pale purple short-sleeved shirt, khaki pants, and two-tone shoes; holding on to a wheelchair.

Joe looks at the smiling man and then at the chair.

"Yes, it's yours."

"You've got to be kidding. I came back as a cripple? Why not is a whiny little girl?"

"That is not a bad idea, I wish had thought of it."

"Did you pick this body?"

"No. I could think of a thousand things worse than this, but the man you replaced is very well liked and respected in his community. Much like you were when Connie was alive."

"What are you talking about? You don't know anything about me or my wife."

"Yes, I do. I know everything about your life on Earth, and if you ask me, you're better off upstairs. Now get up, we have a busy day ahead of us."

Angrily Joe throws the covers back.

"Striped pajamas? I can't wait to see the rest of my wardrobe."

Joe tries to get up, but his legs won't move. He lays there not knowing what to do. Haig steps to the bed and puts his hands under Joe's knees, he then pulls his legs over the side of the mattress. With the help of the crazy golfer Joe manages to get into the chair.

"Your name is Robert Duncan. You teach math and coach basketball at the local high school, and if you don't hurry, you'll be late."

Joe sits in the chair not moving.

"Put your hands on the wheels and push down."

"I know how to do it."

"Don't sit there looking at me, hurry and get dressed, we have to get going. Tick – tock, tick – tock."

Joe pushes himself to an open closet door. The clothes are hanging low enough they can easily be reached from a wheelchair. All are casual, not one suit among them. Joe is amazed at how anyone can go through life without one suit; preferably black.

The light blue short-sleeved polo shirt appears to be the least offensive selection. Replacing the pajama top with the shirt is easy enough, but removing the bottoms presents a number of challenges. He cannot use his legs to raise his butt off the seat to enable him to pull the PJ bottoms down.

If he uses his hands to lift himself up, he has no way to pull the bottoms off. After struggling in vain for several minutes he slaps the chair arms with the palms of his hands.

"How about a little help here!"

"Sorry, I don't do candy striper. Coach Duncan has been in that chair for three years and has become quite efficient at doing everything for himself."

"I'm not Coach Duncan, and I've only been doing this for 15 minutes."

"You'll get better with a little practice. I make a mean cup 'a coffee. Want some?"

Joe glares at the back of the retreating man.

"I thought you were here to help me."

Haig answers from the next room.

"I'm here to make sure you don't do something stupid, not change your drawers."

"Thanks a lot."

Joe studies his predicament.

"I have to remove my PJ bottoms and put on a pair pants, and I'm unable to move anything below my waist. HAIG! I NEED HELP."

Walter remains in the kitchen whistling "I did it my way."

Realizing that his pleas are being ignored Joe studies the dilemma he is in. He has been solving problems his whole academic life, this one is minuscule compared to some others he has contended with. Twenty-three minutes later he wheels into the kitchen where a cup of coffee and a grinning Heavenly Guide is waiting.

"I see you finally got yourself dressed."

"With no help from you. I had to lean to the left side and pull the PJ's down past my butt, then I did the same thing on the right side. Pulling the trousers on was more difficult, but I did it."

"I knew you could do it, all you needed was a little patience. You had a problem to solve and I knew that intellectual brain would not quit until it was solved."

The smirk on the face of his charge annoys the once famous golfer. "What is that goofy looking smile for?"

"What?"

"That face you're making. It's irritating."

Joe snickers at the abominable site before him.

"Are you going to wear that out in public?"

Walter steps back holding his hands out palms up.

"What's wrong with what I'm wearing? Besides, no one can see me except you."

"Nothing's wrong with the khaki slacks, but the purple shirt and white patent- leather shoes are a bit much."

"After a few centuries of wearing white, it feels good to don a little color. Besides it's none of your business what I wear; want some breakfast?"

Joe holds up his coffee cup.

"You can have some but this is my breakfast."

"In that case drink up, I don't eat and you don't want to be late on your first day."

"I thought the coach has been at this school for a couple of years."

"He has, but this is your first day."

Joe takes a sip of coffee.

"You don't eat, but you drink coffee?"

"It's my one desire that I indulge in whenever I am in the human world. Come on now, quit stalling; get with it."

Joe takes another sip.

"I don't know anything about teaching high school."

"You're a law professor, how hard can it be?"

"I won't know any of the names of the teachers or students. I don't even know where my class room is."

"Don't worry about it because you will have the same knowledge and memories the coach had. When people look at you, they will see him, but when you talk it will be from both of you. There will be no Joe or Bobby; it will be both as one."

Joe looks away staring at the wall. He sits quietly rolling himself toward the door.

Walter follows saying:

"I'm driving." Then he snickers.

Walter opens the door allowing Joe to exit the house. While Joe uses the ramp, the guide descends the steps to get in front, and rushes to open the side door of a van sitting by the curb. When he pushes a button that is mounted on the inside of the door frame a section of the floor disengages and lowers to the street providing a platform for Joe and his chair.

"It's better if you back on to the lift and go back as far as you can."

After Joe follows his guides' advice a bar pops up in front of his front wheels. The lift then raises, hoisting Joe and his chair into the van.

"Did this belong to...what did you call him...Bobby?"

"In a way. His was rigged so that he could drive himself, but there isn't enough time for you to learn how to use all the gadgets, so I will be doing all of the driving."

"Since no one can see you how do we explain the fact that I am the only one in the van and I am driving from the passenger side?"

"We don't have to explain anything because it will appear that you are behind the wheel. Neat trick isn't it?"

"That's not so surprising for an angel."

"Guide! I'm not an angel, I'm a guide."

6

Jefferson high is a relatively moderate-sized high school, but it is nowhere near the magnitude of the campus he is familiar with. The similarity is like moving from a castle to a studio apartment. The ornate carving on the building suggests that it is fairly old. Carved pillars on either side of the front doors and the polished stone steps leading up and through the front door is an entrance reminiscent of the buildings built in the late nineteen forties.

Wings on either side of the original structure were probably added in the 1960s. Behind the parking lot on the left side can be seen an even newer football field with a track. Jefferson is a typical middle-class high school.

Walter pulls into one of the parking spots reserved for faculty and sweeps his arms in a huge arc.

"Welcome to your new life. You're going to love it, so hop out… so to speak."

Joe turns his chair toward the side door. Walter pushes a button and it opens. The lift lowers automatically taking his chair to street level.

Wheeling forward Joe calls over his shoulder.

"Are you coming?"

"Of course. I would not leave you alone at a time like this, besides I can't wait to see you in action."

"Yea…well let's go in."

Walter passes Joe and is halfway across the parking lot, as Joe awkwardly follows. He gets to the bottom of the steps and finds that Haig is waiting.

"Whew! This… isn't… as… easy… as…it… looks." Joe pauses to catch his breath." Do you think you could help me up the steps?"

"You forget; no one can see me. How do you think that would look? It would be pretty spooky."

"Just pull one of your Angel tricks and no one will be the wiser."

"Management doesn't like for us to use our 'Angel tricks' too often, why don't you use the ramp at the side door?"

"There's a ramp? Why didn't you say so?"

Walter smiles. "I just did."

THE MULLIGAN

"Fine!"

Joe pushes down hard on the wheels and spins toward the side door. When he gets to the top of the ramp the door opens and Haig is standing there holding it with a huge smile as Joe pushes past.

His first day goes well. Joe knows where his classroom is, and the names of all his peers and their families without having to ask. He can point out which of the students are troublemakers and which ones enjoy school, which is confusing, and a little scary. Going down the hall everyone he passes, students and faculty, smile and speaks to him. Apparently, Coach Bobby is well-liked. This is encouraging. It may not be as bad as he originally thought.

Joe pauses in the middle of all the pleasantries when he spots a blonde vision coming toward him. She has big green eyes, and a most captivating smile with dimples on each side. He feels like he should know her; and, he thinks, pretty well, but her name eludes him.

"Hello Bobby."

"Hello – – – Ms. Harrison."

The blonde stops in front of him, bends over, and places her hand on his chest. With those captivating green eyes gazing into his she whispers, "Since when do you call me Ms. Harrison?"

Joe's face turns red.

"Evelyn."

Evelyn removes her hand and saunters on down the hall. Joe turns his chair around. She looks just as good from the back.

She shouts as she continues walking.

"Give me a call Bobby."

Joe's mind is racing. "Boy, I would like to know her better."

Haig lays his hand on Joe's shoulder.

"For a while you did. The two of you dated."

Joe flinches, and then continues down the hall to his classroom.

"I forgot you were here Haig."

"Apparently you forgot everyone was here."

"So, you can read my mind."

"Just one of my 'Angel tricks'.

"That's one I wish you didn't have."

"What's the matter do you have some thoughts rambling around that you're ashamed of?"

"I just don't like the idea of someone inside of my head."

"Don't worry, I won't tell anyone what I hear."

The guide and his ward continue to Coach's classroom. Joe is surprised that it is so large. He pictured a tiny space full of desks and chairs with a little room for the instructor's desk.

There was plenty of elbow room for the students to move around

Joe turned to his companion.

"It was uncanny. I had no idea who that gorgeous woman was, and then her name suddenly pops into my head."

"She and Bobby had a thing for a while but she wanted more out of the relationship than he did, so they broke up."

"I think she still has feelings for him."

"It does seem that way doesn't it?"

"I think I'm going to like it here."

7

Joe made it to the last class of the day and instead of being agonizing as he expected, it turned out to be relatively enjoyable. His nerves are no longer on edge, and his confidence is riding high. The fear that he was going to screw up is gone, but the tension takes its toll. The muscles in his shoulders are tight and there is the beginning of a headache over his right eye, but this is starting to feel more like it is his life; the only one he ever had. A frightening feeling overwhelms him. He has a sensation that his old life is slipping away.

While he is writing assignments on the chalk board a girl walks in that makes his heart skip a beat. She has grown a lot in ten years but still has his little girl's smile. Joe can't get over what a beautiful woman his daughter has become.

THE MULLIGAN

Samantha is not quite as tall as her father, and she has her mother's gorgeous looks.

She is definitely her mother's daughter; elegant and vibrant. As she winds her way between the desks with the grace of a gazelle, she speaks to everyone she passes.

Joe pulls his eyes away to stare at the chalkboard. He is looking at the words in front of him but he sees nothing. His mind is racing, thinking of what he is going to say to her.

"Hello Samantha, it's your old dad. Hi Samantha it's me, your father. Samantha, you won't believe this but…"

"No she won't! That's why you are not going to tell her."

Joe turns his head and is hit a solid blow with a putter.

"Ouch."

Rubbing his head, he feels a small bump rising. He stops himself from cursing the wielder of the weapon that caused his pain and glances around. No one seems to notice the action taking place in the front of the room.

"Now that I have knocked some sense into you, remember that I can take you back any time I choose."

"Don't do that again."

"What, this?"

The putter lands on his shoulder this time.

"STOP IT!"

The words resound around the room. Everyone freezes where they are and looks at Joe.

"Uh… take your seats."

Joe glares at his attacker and then turns back to the chalk board. How could it hurt for his daughter to know the truth? Surely, knowing her father has returned won't change the world. Granted, if someone killed Hitler the fate of millions could change, but possibly for the best.

There must be a way to talk to his little girl without getting beat over the head. Sooner or later his chance will come.

He makes it through the eighth period math class without blurting out once that he is Samantha's father. He calls on Samantha six times and she answers every question correctly. His pride is bursting; if only he could tell her. He wheels his chair around.

"We only have a couple of minutes left. Does anyone have any questions?"

A hand goes up.

"Yes Samantha?"

"Coach, do you think we will win tonight?"

Every eye turns to the man in the wheelchair in front of the class. This is a question that he wasn't expecting. Searching for an answer; he doesn't have a clue as to what she is referring.

Haig bends down, and whispers into his ear.

"You are also the basketball coach."

Of course, there's a basketball game tonight. He racks his brain trying to come up with a good answer, but he is a complete blank.

"With a team like we have, how can we not?" The words slip out, surprising him.

The sound of the buzzer ending the eighth period and the school day, is drowned out by the cheers.

8

The elation Joe felt after seeing his daughter has been replaced by anxiety and dread, and he is on the brink of panic. It is getting closer to time for the game to start, and he is in his bedroom trying to decide what to wear.

If it were a formal dinner party, or a fund-raising event there would be no problem. He has lectured before packed galleries, and rubbed elbows with dignitaries of several nations, including his own without hesitation, but now he is becoming physically ill. He doesn't have a clue as to how he is going to help those boys win, and he does not know the appropriate attire for a sporting event.

THE MULLIGAN

"What am I going to do Haig? I don't know anything about basketball. What could I possibly tell those boys without looking like a complete idiot?"

The Haig is standing in the middle of the room lining a driver up with the ball. He takes a couple of practice swings, and SWOOSH. Using his club like a walking cane he leans closer to Joe.

"YOU, don't tell them anything. This is the time for you to step back and let the coach take over. His thoughts are with you, so let him take control. He is really a good coach."

Joe absentmindedly moves clothes from one side of the closet to the other.

"How do I do that? Come on coach, step up and do your thing." Joe hesitates a couple of seconds. "Coach, are you there?" Scowling he continues to flip clothes, "he doesn't seem to want to play."

SWOOSH!

"Stop being such a pompous ass Joe. Relax and he will come out."

Joe tilts his head, shuts his eyes, and remains motionless. He opens one eye after about five seconds.

"Nope, nothing, nada, zip. I don't think it's going to work."

"It will, when you need it."

"That's all I've heard since I got here. 'Relax, don't worry, have faith,' but you're not the one that has to face those kids."

SWOOSH!

"Careful! You almost hit me."

"I know! I think I'm turning the club to the left on the swing. Let me try that again."

"I don't have time for this." Joe dons a white shirt with thin black stripes, and a pair of navy-blue pants before heading for the door. "Are you driving, or am I?"

"I'm not going to let you drive, you can't even walk."

"Very funny."

As they enter the school doors, he is amazed at the amount of people gathering in the gym for the game. It is still an hour before the start and the bleachers are half-full. He has never been a sports person, and in fact he has never attended a sporting event of any kind. The thought of sweaty bodies pounding against each other bent on causing pain to the other and chasing a ball around the floor seems disgusting, and at best frivolous to him. Now here he is about to enter the arena and lead his gladiators; hopefully to victory.

Winding his way across the floor, dodging fans, and waving as his friends and neighbors call his name (actually coach's name) does have a euphoric effect on him. He is beginning to think that perhaps he can pull this off, after all he knows everything the coach knew, isn't that what Haig told him?

THE MULLIGAN

Joe starts to the boy's locker room but his path is
obstructed by throngs of bodies milling and jumping, eager for
the game to start. He swerves left and stops, then veers to the
right and stops.

By veering and swerving, starting and stopping, he makes
it through the menagerie and pauses in front of the locker room
door before entering.

Haig, standing behind his chair, pats him on the shoulder,
and whispers in his ear.

"You're going to do just fine. Coach Bobby has the ability
to take the team all the way to state."

"I know Haig! But – – –"

"There are no butts, you can do it. These are your biggest
rivals; you can't just give up. Keep telling yourself, we can't lose
this game."

"I've never even been inside a locker room before; how
can you ask someone that knows absolutely nothing about the
sport, coach a basketball team?"

"Stop saying that. It doesn't matter if you don't know,
Coach does. Let him do the talking. If you rely on Coach's
abilities, everything will work out."

Joe takes a deep breath and pushes his wheelchair
forward, through the doors. The team is dressed and sitting on
benches waiting for him. All eyes are on him as he rolls to the
center of the room.

"I know you guys are the best team in the state.
You…uh… you can beat… who is it we are playing tonight?"
Several voices sing out in unison.
"The Tigers!"

"That's right, the Tigers. The Tigers aren't mean. In fact,
they are just little pussycats. We are the mean ones, we're…
WE'RE… WE ARE…"

The entire team in unison.
"THE WILDCATS!"
"That's right we are the Wildcats, and they are…"
"The Tigers."
"No, they are the pussycats. Now! We are the…"
"WILDCATS!"
"And they are the…"
One boy's answer is barely above a whisper.
"Tigers."
"NO! They are the…"
The entire team answers.
"PUSSYCATS!"
"You don't sound like Wildcats."
"GRRRRR!"
"That's better. Who is meaner, Wildcats or pussycats?"
"WILDCATS."
"Now let's get out there and show those pussycats how to
play round ball."

THE MULLIGAN

The players run from the room screaming and roaring. From the back of the room comes the sound of applause. Joe turns his chair so that he faces the direction of the sound. Haig is sitting on the back of one of the benches with his feet on the seat.

"Very good Joe, or should I say coach?"

"That was good wasn't it? I don't know what happened. I just knew what to say without thinking about it."

"Now that you know you have it in you, get out there with your team and win a ball game."

Joe follows the team and wheels himself through the locker room doors. He is overwhelmed by the orderly chaos surrounding him; the loud fans, the band, and his team doing warm-up drills, engulf his senses.

Joe rolls himself to the home team side as silence falls over the gym. Everyone except Joe stands and faces the flag. He sits erect and places his hand over his hart as the national anthem is played over the loud speakers, and when it ends a loud roar vibrates the walls. The buzzer sounds the start of the game.

Excitement building up inside him Joe calls his boys in and as they gather together, he looks into the eager faces surrounding him; the coach steps up again.

"Everyone knows what to do. You have done this a thousand times. Just go out there and do your best and you will win."

Joe turns to Jim, a tall good-looking athlete.

"OK, captain, let's do it."

Everyone puts their hand into the circle and as they raise them into the air they shout as one:

"WILDCATS."

The team takes the floor; all but Jim who runs over to the sidelines. He gives one of the girls a kiss and then joins the others. Joe tries to see which girl he kissed, but she is hidden in the multitude of fans.

The two teams seem to be evenly matched as they take turns scoring. That is until just before halftime when the Tigers steal the ball and get a basket. Jim gets the ball back and dribbles down the floor, here is a chance to tie it up again. He goes in for a lay-up, and misses. The Tigers bring the ball down court and as they shoot the player is fouled. The ball goes in and is counted. The fouled player sinks one of the of the free throws and the first half ends.

9

The Wildcats enter the locker room a lot quieter than they exited. Some of them are angry, some depressed, and a few have a so-what attitude. Joe needs to come up with something brilliant to say, but the only thing that pops into his head is a poem, The Jabberwocky, by Lewis Carroll.

He loves the way Mr. Carroll used words that are fun to say. Jubjub Bird and Bandersnatch. No one knows what either of those are, but the names conjure up images of mythical beasts. Ones that change each time the poem is read.

Joe slaps himself in the head.

"No! No! No! A brilliant poem, but not what I need now. Why didn't I pay more attention to sports? Coach, where are you?"

None of the team looks up when he enters. All eyes are diverted elsewhere, waiting for the tirade that is sure to come but Joe's voice is soft and calm.

"Not long ago I screwed up. It wasn't my fault; it wasn't anybody's fault it just happened. Well, maybe it was partially my fault, but I lost someone that was dear to me, someone I loved more than anything in the world. After she was gone, I felt sorry for myself, so I tried to dull the pain by drinking. In the process of killing myself I neglected the only other light in my miserable existence. My daughter. Someone that was depending on me to protect her, and I let her down. One day something happened, and I thought I would never get a chance to see her again.

"Then I met an old pro golfer. He was a pain in the ass, is a pain in the ass, but he told me of a redeeming option. It's called a mulligan; a golfing term. A mulligan is a second chance to redo something, to make it right.

We have a mulligan here. We can mope around feeling sorry for ourselves, or we can grab this opportunity and correct our mistakes. We're only down by five points and we have half a ballgame to make it up.

No, wait a minute, forget that we have played half of a game. This is not the second half, it is a whole new game, so go out there and play like it. ARE WE WILDCATS OR PUSSYCATS?"

THE MULLIGAN

"WE'RE WILDCATS!"

"I can't hear you."

"WE'RE THE WILDCATS!"

From the back of the room Joe here's a SWOOSH, and then he leads the team back on to the floor. The second half is unlike the first. His team play like the winners they are. Jim brings the ball down court and passes it to Kevin who sinks a three-pointer. The Wildcats are ecstatic, but it is short lived because the Tigers come back with two points of their own. This appears to be a repeat of the first half with both teams taking turns scoring, until one of the Tigers slaps Jim in the face as he goes up for a shot.

The attempt misses the basket but when he steps up to the free-through line he puts both through the hoop cutting the Tigers lead to three. Joe calls for a time-out. The boys surround their coach eager to hear what he has to say.

"Men, we are only down by three. The Tigers are a good team, but we're better. I know you don't feel like it right now, so this team needs some Razzle Dazzle.

A few snickers pop-up.

"We'll razzle them with our footwork, and dazzle them with our ball passing. I think the Buffalo Shuffle should do it. Has anyone heard of it?"

No one answers.

"It's a favorite ploy used by con-men to cause confusion by the use of misdirection. They get you to look one place while they steal your purse from the other. That is called the Buffalo Shuffle.

We're going to confuse the Tigers by passing the ball back and forth until we get an opening and then make a basket. The passes have to be fast and accurate, and you must never stop moving. We need to keep the Tigers confused and off balance. Everyone has to keep his head in the game if this is going to work."

Joe draws the play on his board.

"Jim brings the ball down and passes to Frank. Will sweeps around, picks it up and passes to Donnie who swings down here and passes to Eddie. He comes through here and passes to Albert. This continues until there is a chance to pass it to Kevin who makes the three pointer, which will tie the game and give us a chance to win in over time."

The boys head back onto court and Walter appears in front of Joe.

"Buffalo Shuffle?"

"It just popped into my head."

The play goes as planned until Kevin's shot is deflected by a Tiger and hits the backboard without going in, Jim gets the rebound and passes it to Kevin who puts it in for three points tying the game.

THE MULLIGAN

The Tigers pass the ball around trying to run the clock down before they take their shot. Jim sees that they are setting up a play for their star shooter to get the ball, and positions himself close to the six-foot four Tiger.

He knows there is no chance to take the ball away, so when the pass is made Jim steps in front and steals it, bringing it back down court. The Wildcat fans are on their feet. None of the Tigers are close enough to stop him so he goes in for an easy lay-up and the two winning points. The buzzer goes off seconds after the ball slides through the hoop ending the game.

The building shakes from the excitement of the fans. Joe is engulfed in the throng filling the gym floor. All the bodies press so tightly together it makes it impossible for him to find the captain to praise him for his leadership and his total points. He gets to do that inside the locker room amid a lot of shouting and cheering.

"You did a great job today Jim."

"It was the team Coach. They're a great bunch of guys."

"Yes, they are, but your leadership and total points had a lot to do with it. I saw you kiss a girl before the game, is she waiting for you?"

"No, I'm going with the team to celebrate; I'll see her tomorrow."

"I thought I would get to meet her, but some other time I guess."

On the ride home Joe feels like he has never felt before. He is riding high on the ecstasy that overwhelms him. The day he was promoted to departmental head was an exciting time in his life but it doesn't compare to the way he feels now.

Haig turns toward Joe from the driver's seat.

"You did a good job today Joe. I knew you would."

"I did, didn't I? I didn't know winning a sporting event could be this exhilarating. In fact I didn't know anything could be."

10

Joe rides the weekend on a cloud. The Haig still hits the imaginary golf balls but none of them come close to Joe's head. Several times he slaps Joe on the butt and says "great job coach," but the crazy antics of his companion doesn't dampen Joe's mood.

The following school day the entire school is jubilant. Classes are easier, the students and faculty happier, and even the administrators are walking on air. When Samantha stops Joe in the hall his already elated emotions fly to the heavens.

"Coach, my aunt wants me to ask if you would like to come to dinner on Thursday."

"Me?"

"Yes why, didn't you like the meatloaf last week?"

"Well, uh…yes I did."

"It doesn't have to be meatloaf; she makes the most fantabulus stuffed pork chops you have ever eaten. Do you like pork chops?"

"Yes, yes I do. As a matter of fact, they're my favorite dish."

"Great! I'll tell Aunt Gertie you'll be there around six, OK?"

"Yes, six will be fine."

Samantha continues down the hall and Joe spins his chair in a circle several times while he repeats the same word, "WOW!"

"I thought you said you didn't like her Aunt Gert, Joe."

Startled, Joe stops spinning. Haig is standing in the middle of the hall wearing black golf cleats, knee socks, tan short pants bloused below the knee, and a light blue shirt with a cardigan sweater. All of which brings a smile to Joe's face.

"What?"

"Nothing." Joe lets a little chuckle slip out before continuing.

"I didn't say I didn't like her, I said I didn't want her raising my child. Once you got past all of the tattoos and the rings everywhere, and I do mean everywhere, she was quite enjoyable to be with. Besides, I'm going so that I can have dinner with my daughter."

"Of course, you are. So, you found her quite enjoyable. You liked her, didn't you?"

"Not at first. I couldn't imagine why Connie would befriend a social outcast such as her. With her Gothic clothes and black lipstick, she could never attend any of our dinner parties, or any of the many functions we were required to either host or make our presence. Not that she ever wanted to."

"You thought she wasn't good enough to go to a dinner party?"

"I don't mean she wasn't good enough; I mean the way she looked and acted was a bit of an embarrassment to me, but not Connie.

"I don't know if Connie liked shocking the intellectual community with Gert's behavior, or possibly she wished she could be like her. Whatever the reason, Connie liked being around her. She enjoyed her rebellious antics and so did I, to a certain extent."

"But not around your intellectual friends."

"Exactly!"

"You were quite a snob weren't you."

"No, I wasn't. There is a time and place for everything, and she didn't know how to control her actions. The one and only time she attended one of our dinner parties, to which I adamantly objected, she sat on the lap of the of the Dean of Admissions and told him she had been bad and needed to be spanked. That is not appropriate any time."

"Ha-ha! But it is funny."

"It wasn't to Dean Hargrove, or his wife."

"So why are you going to her house for dinner?"

"Samantha asked me, well she asked Coach Bobby, so I'm going to see her."

"You're getting into dangerous water here Joe."

"What am I supposed to do?"

"Just be careful of what you say and do."

"I haven't done anything wrong yet have I?"

"No, not YET."

11

Joe changes his mind about going several times before Thursday. At home in the evening, he decides not to go, but when he sees Samantha at school he can't wait for Thursday.

The momentous day arrives; Joe looks at himself in the dresser mirror several times making sure everything is perfect. The person looking back at him still looks like Joe, but there is something different. The eyes are still blue, and the forehead wrinkles between his eyes are still there. His hair and full beard are still dark, but there is a little more gray. Still, there is something different. He can't quite put his finger on it, but there is something.

A photo of Coach Bobby and a blond woman adorns one corner of the dresser. Joe noticed it earlier but now he picks it up and examines it more closely.

The coach looks several years younger than he would now, and he is sporting a thin mustache Haig says he no longer has. Holding the photo up next to his reflection Joe studies both trying to imagine the younger face over his.

The face would be smoother and younger. The hair would be lighter, browner, and no gray. The thin, more pointed nose, would replace his broader, thicker one. The eyes---they are the same. Joe leans closer to the mirror, his eyes are still blue, but the shape has changed. They are smaller, and the wrinkles on the corners are gone. His mouth has also changed, it is smaller. Joe lays the photo face down on the dresser and continues staring at this strange person looking back at him.

"Haig, who do you see when you look at me?"

"I see you."

"You don't see the coach?"

"I wish I did; he's better looking."

"Do I look like---uh---have I changed in any way?"

"I don't know. What are you talking about?"

Joe backs away from the dresser and turns toward Walter.

"Who is the blond with the coach in the photo?"

Haig is lying on the bed with his hands behind his head staring at the ceiling.

"In the photo, Haig, who is the woman?"

"His wife."

"Coach is married?"

"She died a few years ago."

"How many years?"

"Three or four I believe."

"Isn't that about how long he has been teaching here?"

"Yes, about that."

"You never did say how he lost the use of his legs."

Walter continues to stare, and hesitates before answering.

"It was a car accident."

"What happened?"

"Why are you interested?"

Joe re-positions himself in the chair.

"If I'm going to be him, I should know what happened to him."

Haig sits up, pausing to consider his words before answering.

"He had lost his job teaching history in a high school up north. The school lost some funding and since he was the newest teacher he was let go. He had been out of work for six months when this position came open. He applied for it and got it. He and his wife Brenda went out to celebrate and Brenda was driving home because Bobby was to inebriated to get behind the wheel.

"About a half mile from their house the road cuts through a small patch of woods and makes a sharp left turn. Going into the turn she swerved to miss a deer but hit a tree and died instantly. He wasn't wearing a seat belt so he went through the windshield, and was thrown ten yards from the car landing on a large rock breaking his back. He lived, but he was paralyzed from the waist down."

"So, he was in the chair when he came here."

Haig stands and walks, as he swings his club he talks.

"It took him a year before he was ready to return to work. The year of rehabilitation healed him physically to a certain extent, but not emotionally; that took a lot longer."

"I'm surprised they held the position open for that long."

"They didn't. Another one opened at the same time he was released which he reapplied for, and got it."

"Amazing! What are the odds of that happening? A million to one, two million to one? I don't suppose there was any Heavenly intervention, was there?"

Haig looks at Joe with a blank expression on his face.

"How would I know? I'm just a guide."

Joe chuckles.

"Sorry, I forgot."

Joe reaches over and smooths the bed covers where Haig had been lying.

"Coach isn't what anyone would call handsome, but I suppose he is a little attractive, NOT TO ME, but I'm just saying maybe to a woman."

"Are you talking about all women Joe, or one particular woman?"

"I don't know Haig, I guess all women."

"Um…yes of course you do."

SWOOSH!

"Will you stop that? It's getting on my nerves. Why are you always doing that? Did you really make a million dollars playing golf?"

"Yes, I did, and I spent it. I always said that I didn't want to be a millionaire, I just wanted to live like one, and I did."

"I didn't know professional athletes made that kind of money in the old days."

Walter flinches at the word "old."

"We were paid well, but considered lower class. I played professional golf when we were considered a class below the bus-boys, forbidden to enter the front door of the club house."

"You've got to be kidding. I didn't know anything like that ever happened. What year was that?"

"It was nineteen twenty something."

"Didn't it bother you to be treated that way?"

"I hated it and every time I played; it ate at my guts. When we were allowed in the clubhouse, we had separate locker rooms, because they thought it incomprehensible that someone in our station would use the same facilities as their members. One time I was in a tournament in London and was told to enter the club house in the rear.

"I finally got fed-up with being treated that way so I hired a Rolls Royce and footman, I parked it outside the front door of the club house and used it to change clothes. I never entered the club house while playing there."

"I'll bet that didn't go over very well."

"The club administrator called the police and tried to force me to move the car, but I wasn't breaking any laws so there wasn't anything the Bobbies could do. That embarrassed the hoity-toity club members and therefore they were mad as hell. They came close to barring me from playing the game. If it hadn't been for my notoriety, I probably would have been kicked out forever.

"Another time I refused to go into the club house and receive my winnings because earlier they wouldn't let me in to use the locker room, not even the back door. I suppose they were still angry about the Rolls Royce fiasco."

"I can imagine that really enraged them. What happened?"

"The newspapers picked it up and touted me as being a flamboyant character and unprofessional. This perception followed me for the rest of my career."

"I know things changed because athletes are not treated that way now. When did the change take place?"

"Not right away. Other players started objecting to the way we were treated, and I suppose the establishment was afraid there would be an all-out rebellion, but it was several more years before we even started receiving the recognition we deserved."

"So, you changed the way professional golfers are perceived?"

"I may have helped."

"Now I understand why you are such a pain in the ass."

12

Joe has no trouble finding where his daughter and Gertie live because Samantha gives detailed directions. Surprisingly it is in an up scaled neighborhood. It isn't what he calls high class, but close to it. The house is two story and totally brick, on about one acre of ground. The yard, like all others surrounding it, has recently been mowed and free of all weeds.

He parks in front of a three-car garage on what appears to be a slate drive. Before he is completely out of the van Samantha runs out of the house to assist, much to Joe's delight.

"You look lovely Samantha."

"Thank you, but you don't have to be so formal coach. Call me Sam like you do in school. Did you have any trouble getting here?"

"Yes Sama---Sam, I did have a little trouble. I turned a little early a couple of times, but I made it."

THE MULLIGAN

Sam giggles as she pushes Joe's wheelchair towards the back and up a ramp to a deck that runs the entire length of the house. Three French doors along the brick wall provide three separate entrances to the house. Sam stops in front of the center one.

"Can you get the door coach?"

"Of course, a gentleman always opens doors for ladies."

Sam smiles as she pushes him across the threshold and into the living room.

Once inside, Joe is astounded by the vastness of the interior. The house is an open concept which gives the impression that it is larger than it actually is. The dining room, kitchen, and living area has no walls to separate them. It is one large room with vaulted ceilings.

He assumes the bedrooms are at the top of the curving red oak staircase that is directly across from him beside the front entrance door.

He can hear sounds from the kitchen which is across the room and to his right. The clamor is that of someone cooking, but the source of the noise isn't visible.

"Aunt Gert! Coach Bobby is here."

"Dinner is almost ready Bobby; I hope you're hungry."

"I'm starving."

The woman that stands up from behind the island in the kitchen doesn't look like the Gertrude Brukman that he knows. This woman is attractive, not the Gothic chick he remembers. He is struck by her uncanny resemblance to Connie, and wonders why he didn't notice it before.

"The bread has another three minutes in the oven, but go ahead and find a place at the table. Did you have much trouble finding our house?"

"I normally have to go somewhere several times before I can return without trouble but Sam's directions were explicit. I only made one wrong turn; well, maybe two."

This gets a laugh out of Sam and her aunt.

"Seriously though, you shouldn't have gone to so much trouble with this dinner for me."

"It wasn't any trouble. Everything I fixed is easy to prepare, and besides, I love to cook. Sam, I forgot a coffee cup, would you get another one please?"

Samantha takes a cup and saucer from the hutch and places it on the table.

Gertrude enters the dining room with a platter of sliced freshly baked bread.

"The bread is done, so everyone to the table so we can eat."

THE MULLIGAN

The table is set beautifully. Place settings for three using what Joe assumes is Gertie's finest dinnerware. The plates are white China inlaid with gold filigree. Coffee cups and saucers match, as does the soup bowls. The wine glasses and water glasses are crystal with gold rims. The silverware is gold, and gold rings adorn the napkins. A bouquet of roses stands in the center of the table.

Samantha pushes Joe to the head of the table and then follows her aunt to the kitchen to help with the rest of the food. As Sam enters the kitchen Gertie exits carrying a bowl of mashed potatoes and a gravy boat. Samantha returns with green beans and carrots.

"Sit down Sam, I'll get the pork chops."

As she re-enters an aroma drifts in to the dining room that tantalizes Joe's nostrils and causes his saliva glands to double production. Gertie sits the platter of stuffed pork chops in front of him, making it more difficult to restrain himself from digging in before his hostess has taken her seat.

Gertie sits down and she and Samantha take hands and offer their other one to Joe. He puts his hands into theirs and Gertie says grace. She then passes the potatoes to Joe.

"I want to thank you Joe for the flowers. They make a beautiful center piece."

Surprised, Joe glances at Samantha.

Sam smiles and winks.

Returning his gaze to his hostess Joe continues, "I---uh hope you like them."

"I love them."

Joe looks back at Samantha, who stares into her plate about to burst with pleasure. Elated, Joe continues with dinner. He occasionally takes a fleeting look at Sam who appears to be pleased with herself at the way things are turning out.

The food is good, the dinner talk is good, Joe loves being with his daughter and Gertie who is, well, fantastic. The evening is undoubtedly the best he has had in a quite a long time. After dinner they play a game of Sequence. He has never heard of it before, but it isn't long before he catches on to how it is played and finds it enjoyable. After one game to Joe's dismay, Samantha excuses herself to finish some homework. He came hoping to spend time with his daughter, and here he sits alone with the one person that got under his skin so much in the past.

"I don't remember if you told me, but why are you raising Sam?"

"Her mother and father were both college professors, and her mother Connie and I were best friends. Connie died when Sam was small; after that Sam and her father Joe, became very close.

Joe never wanted to remarry but he had several, (she makes the sign of quotation marks with her fingers) girlfriends. No, I wasn't one of them. In fact, Joe was always ashamed of my friendship with his wife."

"I wouldn't say ashamed, I mean I can't imagine anyone being ashamed of you."

"I was sort of a wild child in those days. A bit Gothic with the black clothes, tattoos, and body rings. I didn't like any kind of authority, and I suppose I thought of myself as a free spirit."

"Yes, I can still see that in you but I don't see any rings or tattoos."

"I got rid of all of that when Sam came to live with me. Well, most of it. I still have a couple of tattoos where they can't be seen."

"I can see where a college professor could be embarrassed by that."

"One time Connie asked me to one of their faculty dinners. I was surprised because I was never invited to their dinners. She told me later that Joe was furious but she insisted. She met me at the door and asked me to be nice to her guests. I did. I sat through that entire night listening to their petty discussions about everything and everybody. I bit my lip and didn't say a thing, until this one old biddy asked me why I marked my body up with all those disgusting tattoos and rings.

"She said that I could be pretty if I dressed and acted like a normal person, but the thing that put me over the edge was when she said, and I'll never forget exactly what it was, 'I suppose people like you think this is attractive.' I asked what she meant by people like me and she said, 'you know, lower class.

"Connie looked at me and I could see the hurt in her eyes. Joe was even shocked at what she said, but neither one of them said anything to her. I couldn't say anything either for about a minute, I just sat there in a daze. I couldn't breathe, and everything got blurry. I thought I was going to pass out, but I pulled myself together and glared around the room at everyone, they went on talking as if nothing happened. Anger welled up inside me. Connie saw my reaction and tried to calm me down before I did something drastic.

"She was good at soothing my nerves normally, but it was too late now. Something had to be done.

"I walked over to where the witch's husband sat and plopped down on his lap. I made over him by running my fingers through his hair and shoving his face in my boobs. I don't remember what I said to him but he enjoyed it. The old hag didn't however; she jumped up and yelled at him for sitting there doing nothing. She stomped, with him in tow, toward the front door and left. I was never asked to another dinner."

"I suppose not. What did Connie say to you?"

"She apologized for what the woman said, but she said I shouldn't have done what I did, and then we both laughed about it. I felt bad that I embarrassed Joe. I really liked him, even if he didn't like me so much."

"I'll bet he did like you, but your actions got under his skin."

"No, I'm pretty sure he didn't like me. I overheard him talking to Connie about me. He said that I was socially undesirable."

"He was probably angry about the dinner party."

"He said that before the party. After I blew up and destroyed his dinner, he avoided me entirely. We never saw each other again until Connie's funeral."

"How did he treat you then? I'll bet it was better."

"We really connected. We both lost someone we loved and that created a bond between us. It never became friendship but it did develop into respect; I think. When he passed away Sam had no one to look after her. Connie and Joe's parents were gone and Connie's only brother was single and in the military."

"So, you decided to take control."

"I was Sam's Aunt Gertie what was I to do?"

"You're not really her aunt, you could have walked away."

"No, I'm not her blood relation, but I am her aunt. I was there when she was born, I was there on her first day of school, and I was there when she got her first tutu. Connie was like a sister to me, so I am her aunt.

"Yes, I suppose you are. Why didn't you adopt her?"

"I'm not trying to replace her parents, and I feel it would be a little disrespectful to them."

Gertie stands and smiles while reaching her hand toward Joe.

"Would you like another cup of coffee?"

Joe backs his chair away from the table.

"No thank you I should be going. Tomorrow is a school day and like my students I need a lot of sleep, but I had a great time. The company as well as the food was excellent."

"This was nice. You have a standing invitation any time you want it."

"Be careful what you are saying. I am a horrible cook, so I might make a nuisance of myself."

"Ha, ha! I'll take that chance."

Gertie bends down and brushes her lips against his. It isn't quite a kiss, but it has the same effect on him. Confused about what just happened he pushes himself to the door. Joe pauses with his hand on the knob of the open door. He raises his other hand and rubs the bridge of his nose as he studies the fantastic woman in front of him.

She is nothing like the crackpot he remembers. This Gertrude is elegant, and sophisticated. He always knew she was intelligent and that is what infuriated him so much. He thought she hid her intellectual side behind a rebellious attitude. She is no longer doing that; she has let her full potential emerge. She is beautiful. He reaches over and rubs his thumb across her knuckles, the way he did Connie.

"Good night Gert."

Joe closes the door behind himself leaving Gertrude standing in the middle of the floor. She rises her hand to her mouth.

"Oh!"

"Aunt Gertie is coach Bobby gone."

Gertrude doesn't answer. She is shocked by the way Coach touched his nose and her hand with his finger. Joe had the same habit.

"Aunt Gertie is coach gone?"

"Uh… yes honey he is."

"You like him, don't you?"

Gertrude turns and looks at her ward standing on the stairway.

"Stop playing Cupid and finish your homework."

"I need some help with a math problem. Could you come up here?"

Both adult and child run up the stairs, one growling like a lioness and the other shrieking like a small girl.

13

Walter is driving.

"So that is the infamous Gertie!"

Joe smiles as he watches the buildings zip by. He isn't thinking about the scenery though, it is Gertie that dominates his thoughts. He thought he could never feel this way about another woman after Connie, but here it is. His emotions range from elation to fear.

"She is not the woman I remember. The Gertie I remember was defiant, seditious, and definitely iniquitous."

"I don't know what Gertie was like before or what those words mean, but I do know this woman is – – –"

"Magnificent!"

Walter smiles, "Yes, I suppose she is."

They travel on without either one of them speaking. Each in his own thoughts. Walter is delighted that Joe is in such high spirits. He realizes there is a chance his charge will get carried away and do something stupid, but for now Walter is content to let it slide. For some odd reason he likes this intellectual snob. He is willing to give Joe a little more latitude than his previous charges; much to the chagrin of St. Peter.

Sooner or later, he will have to clamp down on Joe, but not yet. He has empathy for this snobbish human, something Guides are not allowed to do. He can sympathize with a father's desire to protect his daughter, even if it is against the rules. So, for now he's content to let Joe enjoy the moment.

Joe's head is filled with images of Gertrude standing up from behind the kitchen island, wearing an apron and a huge smile, and taking his breath away. Her walking in caring food, radiant as she glides across the floor. Her sitting on the sofa, close enough that he can smell her perfume but because of his chair not close enough that they can touch.

How did Bobby manage to have a relationship with anyone? The physical aspect alone would be daunting, not to mention the mental aspect.

What he thinks most of is the kiss. Her leaning over his chair to sit something on the table beside him. Her face inches from his, giving him the opportunity to lean forward slightly, allowing their lips to touch, sending electric shocks through his body.

It only lasted a millisecond, but the feeling it left in him was unlike anything he has felt since, well, a long time ago. However, Gertie might not have felt the same. She might not have even noticed the kiss; such as it was.

What if she was just being a good host? He knows from experience what a host has to do for a party to go well. The things he has to endure. Could that be it? His host was just that, being a host?

Walter noticed a sudden change in Joe.

14

The Guide and his ward arrive home and get into the house without any conversation. Haig never sleeps, but he vanishes at bedtime. Joe has no idea where to, but he is always back when Joe rises in the morning. He asked Haig about it once, but all the big man said was that being a babysitter wasn't his only job.

The night passes slowly as Joe restlessly tosses and turns in bed. Visions of Gertrude Brukman enter his sleep as dreams, formulating doubts as to whether or not tonight was real. The images that pass before his closed eyes jerking back and forth during the REM sleep, are of a gorgeous, stunning, sexy woman.

She drifts in and out of his sleep fantasies, first as the angelic Aunt Gertrude and then a devilish Gothic rebel sending his emotions on a roller coaster ride.

When daylight does break, the nights long torments subside, and Joe finds himself still reeling from the previous night's dinner. He had gone there with hopes of being with his daughter, but found himself spending the evening with a most amazing woman. Doubts that she sent mixed signals faded, because he didn't want to believe it.

He still can't believe the complete transformation that took place in a few short years into the self-reliant, sophisticated woman she is today. However much he loves to be around Gertie, he still longs to talk to Samantha. There is so much he wants to ask her.

The school day drags on until the eighth period. His actions are robotic, as the day passes in a fog. Joe glances at the clock every few minutes during each class trying to will it to move faster; the excitement and anxiety building to the moment when he pulls his daughter aside as soon as she enters the room.

"Saman… Sam, can I speak to you after class?"

"OK!" She answers, and takes her seat.

It is difficult to concentrate on his lesson plan in anticipation of the talk he is going to have with her. There is so much he needs to say, and so many things he wants to tell her.

THE MULLIGAN

This is what he has been waiting for, and it is why he came back. He doesn't know how he is going to break the news to her, or how she will take it, but he has to let her know who he is.

The ringing bell end's his class and the school day. Joe's heart rate increases and his stomach makes gurgling sounds as his daughter strides to the front of the room.

"You wanted to talk to me coach?"

"Have a seat."

Samantha sits in the first seat and Joe wheels around his desk.

"I enjoyed dinner last night."

"Great! What did you think of my aunt? I know she likes you. Last week things didn't go so well, but I thought last night was a huge success. Did aunt Gertie tell you she is CEO of her own clothing company?"

"No, she didn't."

"Well, she is. She started it up when I came to live with her, and now it's international."

"That is impressive. I wouldn't have thought she was capable of such an accomplishment. She was always so imprudent."

"She was what?"

"Nothing! I just got the impression that she was irresponsible in her youth."

"My dad thought the same as you. He talked about how she made him so angry, but I remember fun times with her and my mother."

"Do you remember your mother?"

Samantha nods her head.

"She was beautiful and smart. She taught me to play the piano, and when I got interested in the violin she took me to lessons. She was happiest when I studied ballet. Aunt Gertie told her that I wasn't a dancer but she insisted I learn, until my first recital, which turned out to be my last. My father even admitted I couldn't do it, and he thought I could do anything."

"He must've loved you very much."

"And I loved him, but he was pretty narrow-minded."

"What do you mean?"

"He thought Aunt Gertie was a kook and he didn't like me being around her, I think he was afraid her actions would rub off on to me. He thought everyone had to conduct themselves in such a way that no one could criticize them. He always worried about doing or saying the wrong thing. You are what people think you are he would say."

Leaning on his elbows Joe bends forward, getting closer to Sam's face.

"He was in a prestigious position that required him to maintain an impeccable reputation, and he thought your aunt's actions would reflect on him…probably."

Joe leans back, and Samantha stands.

"I guess so, but Aunt Gert is completely different from both my mother and father. She does what she wants and doesn't care what people think. I love both my parents, but I want to be like my aunt. I have to go coach, but if you want to see my aunt again, I know she likes you."

"Do you have to leave so soon? I have a lot of questions I want to ask."

"I have to meet my friend."

"A boyfriend?"

"Yes! A boyfriend."

"WHO… uh, do you mind if I ask who he is?"

"No, I don't mind."

"Well, who is he?"

"I said I didn't mind if you ask, I didn't say that I would tell you."

Anger slips in a little, causing Joe's voice to raise a notch.

"Why don't you want me to know who he is? Why is it such a big secret?"

"It's not a big secret, but I just don't want to make a big deal of it."

"I'm not trying to make a big deal; I am just asking."

"I don't want my aunt knowing, OK?"

"I won't tell her if you don't want me to, but why don't you want her to know? Is he some punk rocker or something?"

"No, it's just that whenever I tell her about a boy I like, she goes crazy. She wants to invite him to dinner so she can meet him, and then she makes all kinds of excuses to get the two of us together. It's embarrassing."

"Ha-ha, I see." His voice quiets. "I won't tell her anything."

"I'm afraid you will let it slip and then my life will be hell."

"I won't let it slip; I can control myself."

"I can't take that chance. I have to go now coach. Bye."

Samantha leaves and Joe turns to his specter friend.

"Haig, my little girl has a boyfriend. What am I going to do?"

Haig is slouching in one of the desks casually hitting the soul of his shoe with his putter.

"About what? She's old enough to be serious about a boy."

"As long as he is the right kind of boy."

Walter bounces out of his seat to stand in front of Joe's chair.

"The right kind? And if he isn't the right kind? What do you plan on doing? I hope you're not going to try to break it up."

"I just want to know who he is, and if he is good enough for her. I don't want her throwing her life away on some loser."

"It's not up to you; you're just here to observe remember?"

"You don't expect me to stand by and do nothing if she is dating a hoodlum do you?"

"Yes, I do. That's part of the deal. You just wanted to know how she was doing."

"That's all I want. I need to know who she's interested in, but she's not going to tell me. I guess I could ask some of her friends, or… you know, don't you? Just tell me who he is."

"So you can cause trouble? I don't think so."

"Haig, I have to know. If he is right for her, I won't do a thing, but – – –"

"But nothing. If you try to interfere, I'll be forced to take you back. Do you understand?"

Silence.

"Do you understand?"

"YES! I understand."

15

The first thing Joe does when he gets to school the following day is to ask several students if they know Sam. Those that know her don't know who she is dating, or at least they tell him that. When she gets to his class, he sticks to the class outline and never mentions their talk. He struggles through the remainder the lesson plan and then after the final bell he heads for basketball practice.

"Jim, could I speak to you for a second?"

"Yeah coach, what is it?"

"Do you know Sam Parrish?"

"Yeah, why?"

"I heard that she has a boyfriend and I was wondering… do you know who he is?"

"Why? Is something wrong?"

"No, nothing's wrong, I was just wondering who she is going out with. There's nothing wrong with it, I am just curious that's all."

"She's dating someone? Sorry coach I didn't know she was dating again."

"Again? This isn't her first uh…boyfriend?"

"Are you kidding? Have you seen how hot she is?"

Joe doesn't want to hear that a boy thinks his daughter is hot, but he ignores the statement.

"How many boyfriends has she had?"

"I don't know, two or three. You should ask her, coach."

Jim joins the rest of the team in warm-ups.

It is strange to Joe that no one knows the boy. It is possible that he goes to another school. That would explain the lack of knowledge of this boy by the entire student population. He understands why she has to keep it secret from Gert, but why from him?

Joe wheels his chair around and heads for the corner where Walter is lining up his putt. Dressed in a Hawaiian shirt, orange shorts, and white tennis shoes with white socks Walter makes an unforgettable sight.

Doing his best to control the urge to burst out in laughter Joe is delighted that he is the only one that can see the flamboyant guide.

"The boy is a hoodlum Haig, and she doesn't want Gertie to know. Or, he isn't very bright, OR, he is older and doesn't even go to school. That's it! He is an older man and she knows Gertie wouldn't approve. I've got to find this cradle robber and put a stop to it."

"Calm down Joe. You're letting this drive you crazy. You don't know that he is an older man, in fact you don't know anything about any of this."

"What else could it be? She won't tell anyone anything about him."

"She won't tell you anything about him."

"Yes, well that's because she is ashamed of him."

"You know who she is seeing, what do you think?"

"No, I don't know who he is."

"Of course, you do. Angles know everything. If you won't tell me who he is, at least tell me if he is an older man."

"You have to stop this Joe. You have to let happen what is to happen."

"I don't even know what that means, besides a father does what he has to in order to protect his children. "

"How do you know that what you're going to do is protecting your daughter? What if this boy is the best person for her, and you prevent them from getting together? ""I'm not an angel, besides Angels don't know everything, only God does."

"But you can find out, can't you? St. Peter has a book that can tell him anything. He probably knows which one of my mother's breasts I preferred when I was born. Just look it up."

"It ain't go'na happen Joe."

"Fine!"

Joe spends the next two days quizzing all of the students and faculty on the mystery boy. No one knows anything about him, or if they do, they are not telling Joe. There seems to be a conspiracy involving the entire school. In frustration he decides to confide in the one person he thinks will be sympathetic to his desires. The person he once considered an off-the-wall troublemaker, but now he finds interesting, and beautiful. Tomorrow being Saturday, it will be a good day to call the ex-Gothic troublemaker.

16

When Joe knew Gertrude Brukman, she was the most undesirable person to be around that he had ever known. He never understood what Connie saw in her that made them such good friends. They were as much alike as a tiger and a lamb. The two women were college buddies who became lifetime buddies. Connie concentrated on her studies and maintaining a high grade level while Gertie spent most of her school years at one protest rally after another. He didn't think she knew what she was protesting half the time. She simply enjoyed harassing the establishment and it brought her close to being expelled more than once.

THE MULLIGAN

Her Gothic clothing and piercing caused most people to shy away from her. She was not only obstinate but also a little scary. Gertie's grades and IQ were at the top of her class. It was the only thing that prevented her from being expelled.

If she had conformed and followed the rules, there is no limit to what she could have achieved. She showed up for her classes late, if she showed up at all. She rarely participated in class discussions but when she did her statements were brilliant. Her attitude kept her from becoming Valedictorian which allowed her best friend Connie to receive that honor.

Connie on the other hand followed all the rules and was the perfect wife for Joe. She was beautiful, intelligent, and with as many letters behind her name as an alphabet book. She was a history professor, and the perfect host. Her dinner parties were the epitome of social grace.

Everyone clamored to be invited to dinner at the Parrish's. It was a status symbol. Aside from the ability to mesmerize everyone she met; her smile was reassuring. Connie almost never met a stranger, and every stranger she did meet wanted to be her friend after that meeting. These however weren't true friends.

"Gertie was the only true friend Connie had during her college years, and the rest of her life. There were those that came and left, but the weirdo hippie was there for the duration.

"After school Connie went to work for the Smithsonian but her heart wasn't in it, so she decided to teach. That is when she discovered her first and second love, her love for Joe and her love for the kids. Not necessarily in that order. Sometimes Joe wondered which one was first. When she started at the university Joe had been teaching there for almost a year.

One day he was on his way to confer with the Dean about one of his students when this young woman rounded a corner and crashed into him. She was late to a class and not paying attention to where she was running. He thought she was a student and gave her a verbal lashing before she could apologize for knocking him down. Angered by his tirade she told him, in no uncertain terms, what a portentous bully he was before storming off. Instead of being offended by her, he was enchanted. Determined to find out who this charming lady was, he searched the school in vain.

Purely by accident he discovered that she was not a student, but a highly qualified member of the faculty. He was passing an open class room door when he glanced in and was shocked to find the object of his hunt giving a lecture. The kids were mesmerized by her as much as he was.

That attribute along with a selfless quality is what made it so difficult to go on without her, and why, after she died Joe turned to booze.

THE MULLIGAN

It's true he did lose his way for a while. Promiscuous relations and alcohol did not make him forget; it just prolonged the agony. He tried to be stronger for his daughter, but he always fell back down the rabbit hole. In the end the things he was using to prop himself up were the things that knocked him back down and took away the only light left in his life.

It's not true that Joe was about to achieve everything he wanted in life before he died. He was going to be published again, but his standing in the literary community was deteriorating rapidly. Without Connie by his side Joe could not host the dinner parties with the same elegance and grandeur, so he didn't try.

Invitations to other parties dwindled quickly because he always became inebriated and embarrassed his hosts; soon faculty members started avoiding Joe altogether. The number of students attending his classes dropped dramatically causing concern with the University board.

The fact that he was involved with several of his students added fuel to the fire. Meetings were held trying to decide how to handle "the situation". He was in fact on the edge of termination when the incident that brought him to meet Walter Hagan occurred.

17

Gertrude is on a conference call to London when call-waiting informs her that another call is coming in. Seeing that it is Coach Bobby she terminates the London call telling them that she will call back on Monday.

"Hello, how are you?"

"I'm fine. I need to talk to you."

"Okay, I'm not busy right now. What do you want to talk about?"

"Not over the phone, I want to come over."

"That would be great, how about this evening? Do you think you can get here all right?"

"I'll be there in fifteen minutes. "

Dial tone.

Gertrude stares at the phone.

"He hung up on me."

She has only fifteen minutes to get a lot done. She is still in her PJs, her hair is a mess, and she has no makeup on. The house is in pretty good shape; there are a few things that needs to be picked up but otherwise it looks good. She picks up a blouse and a pair of shoes on her way through the living room. As she gets herself ready to see Bobby her thoughts drift to the two dates they have had. Although Sam thinks of them as dates, she doesn't think they were really dates.

Normally she only dates men that can further her ambition. They are either in the fashion world or are involved with fashion in some way. Bobby is different. He has no interest in fashion whatever, he doesn't even know what it is. She would love to replace his entire wardrobe with something that is not so haphazard. He teaches high school English and coaches basketball; that is a welcome relief from the rat race of her world. He may be just what she needs to balance her life, so maybe these are dates.

That is unless this is a goodbye talk. The first date was not a memorable one. It didn't go that bad, but it didn't go that well either. The other night however was a huge success, at least as far as she is concerned. Perhaps he doesn't think it went all that well. She tries to contemplate what she could have done.

He said he loved the dinner, and that pork chops were his favorite. Afterward they talked about everything for most of the night. There was an awful lot of questions about Sam but he's her teacher, and he seems to care about her.

She can't think of anything that would cause him to stop seeing her. Did she talk too much or too little? Was she too forward when she sat on his lap and then joked about the chair holding both of them? When she leaned over giving him the opportunity to kiss her, was that to brazen? There were so many things that could have gone wrong. What in the world can he want to talk about?

After several knocks Gertie opens the door and Joe's heart rate increases two-fold. She is stunning in her form fitting Capri's and lacy top. Her hair is loose and falls around her shoulders the way it did at dinner the other night.

"Come in Bobby."

Joe hurries past her and into the living room.

This time she sits in a chair across from him, not wanting to take a chance on messing up again.

"What is it that is so important that you needed to rush over and talk to me?"

Joe squirms in his seat.

"Well --- I uh don't know how to ask this."

"Just ask."

"It's about Sam."

"Sam? What's happened to her?"

"Nothing has happened. It's just that I'm worried about her."

"Why? What's wrong?"

"Nothing! At least I don't think so. It's just that she is so secretive."

"About what?"

"Her boyfriend."

"She doesn't have a boyfriend."

"Yes, she does."

"No, if she had a boyfriend she would have told me. We are more like sisters than aunt and niece."

"She does have a boyfriend; she told me so."

Gertie stands up with her hands on her hips.

"But she doesn't. I would know."

She stares at Joe.

"She has a boyfriend? Why would she tell you and not me?"

"She doesn't want you to know."

"Why not? I think it is great, I want her to have boyfriends. Her last two boyfriends, well her only two, came over several times for dinner. I took them to the club, and even got memberships for the boys. I did everything I could to encourage a relationship. I think I liked Jim more than the other one, I can't remember his name."

Jim's name slips past Joe.

"That is a problem, you do too much encouraging. She said, and I quote, 'whenever I tell her about a boy she goes crazy'."

"That's not true. I'm just trying to help. It's difficult for a young girl. If she tries too hard the boy feels threatened, but if she holds back too much, he thinks she is an ice princess. If I orchestrate everything the pressure is off Sam."

"Forget about that, that is not the problem."

"What do you mean forget about it? Sam thinks I'm a busybody and you say it is not a problem?"

"I didn't say it is not a problem, I said it is not the problem that worries me."

"What worries you?"

"The fact that no one knows who this mysterious boy is, not her classmates, teachers, or even her friends. Doesn't that sound strange to you?"

"Just how do you know all of this?"

"I've been asking around."

"You've been asking around? Who do you think you are? What business is it of yours?"

"When one of my best students' grades start going down, I try to find out why. She is too bright to throw her entire future way on some boy."

Gertrude doesn't say anything, her eyes are fixed on the floor. Joe studies the face of this beautiful woman. He can tell she is thinking about what he has just said. When she does speak it is calm and collected.

"You really believe she has a boyfriend?"

"Yes, I do."

"And you think he is the cause of her grades dropping?"

"Yes."

"When would she see him? She never goes out except to a ballgame or other school function."

"Perhaps they meet at the game. Who does she go to the games with?"

"I used to go with her, but lately she has been going with some girlfriends."

"Do you know their names?"

"Not really, for a while she talked about this one girl named Amy, but I haven't heard Sam mention her for some time."

"Amy? Do you know her last name?"

Gertie searches her memory.

"No, I don't think Sam ever told me, but I think she is on the cheer-leading squad."

"Can you think of anyone else?"

"A few years ago, there was this girl, I believe her name was Christie, or Chris☐ie, something like that, but I believe she moved away."

"All right then."

Joe wheels toward the door.

"On Monday I'll find Amy and see if she can tell us anything."

"I'll just ask her when she comes home. She'll tell me."

"No, don't do that. You'll just be butting in again. We have to discover who he is before confronting her. We'll decide what to do then."

"Are you sure we are doing the right thing? Sam is a good girl; I trust her. I don't want to mess up our relationship."

"I know she is a good girl, but sometimes good girls get off on the wrong tracks. They just need a little help from us to see where they are headed.

"If Sam is making a mistake, we'll deal with it. If she isn't and there is nothing going on, we'll figure out what her problem is."

"And if we can't?"

"We will. We have to for her sake. I have to leave now but I intend to come back soon for some more of those pork chops."

"I was about to fix myself some lunch. It would be just as easy to fix enough for two."

"Isn't Sam here?"

"She went to the library to get research on a school project."

"I suppose I could stay long enough to eat. I am pretty hungry and I know what a good cook you are."

18

Walter Hagan is standing outside Gertie's house when Joe leaves. Joe stops short when he sees him.

"What are you doing out here?"

Walter Paces, and as he does, he swings his golf club.

"I had to get away from you."

"Why? What have I done? "

Walter stops pacing and glares a Joe.

"You are a cat's whisker away from going back."

"Because I want to help my little girl, and keep her from ruining her life?"

"Because you are about to break the most important rule you were given."

"Rules! That's all you think about. If you want to take me back for the simple reason that I want to help Sam straighten out her life, then go ahead and do it."

"You are the most exasperating human I have ever had to work with."

"Come on Haig. You know I have to do whatever I can. You would do the same."

Walter studies the man in front of him. The man he has developed a friendship for. Guides are not supposed to get involved with their charges, and certainly not form a camaraderie. Joe is getting in muddy waters and if Walter is not careful, he will be in there with him. St. Peter has already warned him about allowing Joe so much leeway, but Joe is right, if the roles were reversed, he would do the same.

The anguish in Joe's face is difficult to ignore. That, along with the puppy dog look determines the decision Walter is about to make.

"You'll be walking on eggs Joe, break too many and---."

"Thanks Haig. See, I said you are an angel."

"Don't thank me because I might change my mind. I'm responsible for everything you do, so if you get into trouble I get into trouble. The only thing they can do to you is not let you see your daughter again.

For me on the other hand, the consequences would be more dire. They could revoke my guide status. I would never be permitted to leave. Don't get me wrong, I love it there.

Never wanting for anything, playing the game I love whenever and as much as I want. Not having to worry about anything, and no one telling me what to do, except for St. Peter that is.

"The thing I would miss most is my wardrobe. White is a good color, now and then, but not forever. I have such an assortment of outfits with color that I could wear a different one everyday for eternity. I don't want to loose that, so if it comes down to you or me, guess who I'll choose."

"I understand. You'll do what you have to, and I'll do what I have to."

19

Samantha is angry after she talks with coach Bobby. She doesn't know why everyone is meddling in her life. It is no one's business.

"I'm not a little girl anymore; I'm old enough to decide what is best for me."

She doesn't know why she told coach her friend was a boy, it's just the first thing that popped into her head. Why didn't she tell him her friend was a girl? She knows why. It might slip out her name is Chris☐ie.

There is no boyfriend right now. She thought she loved Jim but he took too much for granted; mostly her. He has his life planned out and he assumed she would follow, but she doesn't want to follow anybody's dream but her own.

Right now, her dream is hazy. Once, when mother and father were alive, she knew what it was;.

After high school her plans were to go on to Julliard and study music, mainly piano. One day she would perform at Carnegie Hall. Then she would tour the world playing for huge crowds. She would become a primadonna of the piano. That was the life her parents wanted for her so it was what she wanted also. When her mother died so did her passion for piano, but her father kept pushing her in that direction. He would tell her that her mother was watching from heaven. He insisted she practice for a minimum of two hours every evening. She did as he asked, but the feeling she had for it was gone.

At one time Samantha's fingers would fly over the keys, and a heavenly sound would spill out. Now, since her mother's passing, she struggles, and falters, and hits sour notes.

Her father could not hear it, he heard what he wanted to. He told her "whatever the problem is it will go away if you practice enough." So she practiced longer and harder. The life she once loved had become a horror story, and then her father and the music died. Now that he is not here her future is hazy. The only thing she is sure of is it doesn't include playing the piano professionally.

THE MULLIGAN

With both parents gone she felt alone and frightened.
That is when Aunt Gertie came into her life and brought the
sunshine back. Her aunt is easy-going and definitely
undisciplined. Samantha's old life died with her parents and her
new life began with Aunt Gert.

The days of schedules are gone. When Samantha wakes
in the morning, Other than school, she has no idea what she is
going to do for the remainder of the day. She is happy once
again. Sam misses her parents, but she is thankful for Aunt
Gertie. Her aunt is not as strict as her parents were, but she is just
as annoying sometimes. She is very much a romantic. If Sam
mentions a boy to her that she likes, Aunt Gert immediately
begins making plans to get the two of them together.

Her aunt never married, but she seems determined to see
that Sam does. She loves her, but she is only her aunt, not her
mother. Now coach Bobby is meddling in her life. Why doesn't
everybody leave her alone?

Recently Sam started playing the piano again, but it is
just for fun. There are no long hours of practice, no frustrations
because she can't get the cord just right, and no one nagging her
to try again. She plays now just for the enjoyment the music
gives her. If she hits a wrong note or the tempo is not quite right,
she does not care. This is the way music is meant to be played.

She does not hate her old life because at the time it was all she knew, but that was then and this is now. Aside from the meddling adults, her life is pretty good now except for her problem with Christie. Her anger caused Christie to do something terrible. She should never have lost her cool and said those hideous things, but Christie was acting stupid and would not listen to her.

She does feel bad about keeping her secret from everybody, especially Aunt Gert, but she isn't ready to tell anyone just yet. Maybe she never will.

20

Jim is starting to worry about Sam. He didn't think much about it before coach talked to him, but now that he mentions it, she hasn't been acting like herself lately. She is irritable and secretive; everything seems to set her off. Nothing he does is right. If he agrees with her, he is being patronizing. If he disagrees, he is being a jerk. It isn't just him that sends her into a frenzy, but everyone. Her teachers are upset with her, her aunt is…well she is oblivious to everything that is going on around her, and Coach Bobby is trying to be her dad.

Jim has his life planned out. After graduation he is going to Purdue University in Indiana (his father's old school), and Sam is going with him (or so he thought). He might play ball in school to help with expenses, but pro ball isn't his ambition.

He has been thinking about something in the health field, but not a doctor. It takes too long to become a doctor, and he doesn't want to spend half his life in school.

Perhaps a dentist, or a male nurse, or a medical technician. Any of these professions will provide a good living without so many years of study. After he and Sam graduate, they will establish their careers, and get married; in that order. Later, probably much later, there will be time for kids.

Sam however, doesn't share his enthusiasm for this plan. In fact, she stormed out of his house when he told her. She called him a self-centered moron. She yelled, screamed, and stomped her feet. Before she slammed the door, she threw his class ring at his head and called him an idiot, but she's the one that is acting stupid. She wants marriage and kids right away. Her priorities are all screwed up.

There are places he wants to see, both here and abroad. By combining both of their future paychecks they could have the life of the rich and famous. If they wanted to vacation in Japan or St. Thomas, it would be their choice. Once she starts popping out kids, all life as he wants to know it will vanish.

Well, if she wants to be like that, let her. He'll give her some time to think this over. She'll come back when she calms down, but if she doesn't, then it will be for the best because she would be an albatross dragging him down.

He was shocked when Coach told him she was dating someone else. He can't imagine who it is. The guy must be from another school, because he would know if the dude went to Jefferson.

She's probably doing this to make him jealous. He'll ignore her for a few weeks, and she'll come running back; he knows she will.

21

Walter Hagan, former professional golfer; presently heavenly guide, is standing in front of St. Peter prepared for the dressing down he is sure is coming. He told Joe that time up here has no meaning, but right here right now, that isn't true. It feels like he has been here a lifetime. Peter appears to be concentrating on the book in front of him. Walter clears his throat several times with no visible effect. His boss continues turning pages with an occasional glance up, one eyebrow raised.

Here he is, a man who played golf while leaders of the world watched with admiration; feeling like a schoolboy in the principal's office. He has been here before, but it had been because of his childish pranks. This time however, is more serious.

His eyes wander around while he shifts weight from one foot to the other. Eventually his gaze falls on his shoes. A gasp escapes his lips before he can stop it.

He changed out of his earth clothes before returning because St. Peter is a stickler for dress code. On Earth, away from the strict rules, guides are permitted to dress as they want, but when in the presence of a Seraph everyone is required to dress in traditional Heavenly white. That is how Walter is presently dressed, except for his shoes. He forgot about them; all he can do now is pray that St. Peter doesn't notice.

Closing the book St. Peter leans back in his chair.

"Tell me about Joe."

"What do you want to know?"

"How is he doing? Is he fitting in with the new life? IS…HE…FOLLOWING…THE… RULES?"

Walter takes a step closer to the table in an attempt to hide his shoes.

"Sort of."

"What does that mean?"

"He hasn't crossed the line yet."

"Yet?"

"I don't mean he will. I just mean it's difficult not to interfere when it is your daughter, and you think she needs your help."

"That is why you are there. It is your job to see that he doesn't."

"I know, but if it were my little girl, I would do my best to help her."

"But it isn't. I've given you quite a lot of latitude in the past, and you took advantage of it. This time I'm holding the reins a little tighter. Now do your job and see that this doesn't get out of hand. If you can't handle it I'll put someone else on it that can."

Walter swings his club onto his shoulder and walks away. As he is leaving, he looks back over his shoulder.

"I know what has to be done. I'll take care of it."

"One more thing."

Walter turns.

"Yes?"

"Do something about those shoes."

22

Joe quizzes the entire student body and faculty about Sam's friend Chris□ie. Some know of her, and some know a little, but no one admits to knowing much until he asks Michelle.

"Yeah, I knew her, she was Sam's friend."

At last Joe is getting somewhere.

"What can you tell me about her?"

"She was weird. She wore black clothes and walked around with her head down, never talking to anybody or looking at them. If you said anything to her, not that anyone would, she pretended not to hear you. It was as if she wanted to be invisible."

"She wanted to be invisible? She must have been pretty lonely. No friends to hang with, or anyone with which to talk."

"I guess."

"Is that what made her weird? She wore black and never talked to anyone?"

"That was part of it, but what was really weird was that one-day Darcy said something mean to her. I wasn't close enough so I couldn't hear what it was, but she had been picking on Chris□ie for a week or so. This one day Chris□ie was getting something out of her locker when Darcy and a couple of her friends came up behind her and started making fun of the way she dressed. She pretended not to hear until Darcy whispered something. Chris□ie turned to face the three girls and the look on her face was frightening."

"What do you mean?"

"I don't know, it was as if she turned into a monster. Her eyes were REALLY BIG, I mean HUGE. They were red. But not just red, it was is if this --- you know how in cartoons they shoot little daggers out of their eyes? Well, she was shooting Bowie knifes. She got up close to Darcy, so close that their noses touched and mumbled something, then she stomped off. Darcy just stood there for a couple of seconds; she was clearly scared."

The next day she didn't come to school, and she was out all week. The word was that her face broke out in red bumps and splotches. When she did come back, she wouldn't talk about it. She never told anybody what happened, but she stayed out of Chris□ie's way from then on."

"Do you think Chris□ie caused her face to breakout?" Michelle gave Joe that 'how dumb can you be' look.

"Do you know for a fact that she was responsible?"

"Mona's cousin is best friends with Irene who goes with Darcy's brother Jerry. Jerry told Irene who told Mona's cousin who told her sister Olivia who told Lillian who told Gracie who told me. So, yes, I know for a fact."

Joe shakes his head and smiles.

"That's good enough for me. So how do you think she accomplished this fantastic feat?"

"Duh! She's a witch."

"A witch?"

There is that 'how dumb can you be' look again.

"What did she do, cast a spell on the poor girl?"

"That's what witch's do."

Joe examines the face of the young girl in front of him. She is convinced that Chris□ie is a witch. The whole school probably believes it. Can this be the big secret? Does Sam practice witchcraft also? No, that is impossible. Sam is too intelligent to believe in witches. Isn't she?

"If everybody thinks Chris□ie is a witch why did Sam become friends with her?"

"Sam never believed she was, she was the only one in school who didn't. She felt sorry for her and started talking to her. Then the two began walking down the hall together and sitting at the same table at lunch."

"What did you other kids think about that?"

"We all tried talking her out of it. Sam is well liked by everyone, but she isn't one of the in-crowd. She never wanted to be, but the kids that are kind of admire her because she lives in both. I think she was so friendly with the "Kook" partly because she felt sorry for her, partly because no one else was, but mostly because she enjoyed being the one that crossed the line. Until one day she wasn't."

"They weren't friends anymore? Why not?"

"I don't know, something happened between them. They stopped talking and eating together. If they accidentally met in the hall, they would try to avoid getting too close. This went on for a couple of weeks. Then Chris☐ie stopped coming to school. We heard that her family moved to another state."

"What did Sam say about it?"

"Nothing. She never talked about it."

"How long ago did this happen?"

"I don't know, maybe a year or two."

"Do you think Amy would know anything about it?"

"Amy Singleton? Yeah probably, she wasn't friends with Sam then but maybe Sam talked to her about it."

"Do you know what class Amy is in right now?"

"No, but she will be at cheerleader practice after school."

"Do they practice in the gym?"

"Usually, but not always; sometimes they go out to the football field."

"Thank you Michelle, you've been very helpful."

"Is Sam in some kind of trouble?"

"No, of course not"

"Why all of the questions about her?"

"I heard that she has been different lately. Like something is bothering her. I'm just trying to find out what it is."

"Why would you do that?"

"Her aunt is worried and I'm trying to help."

"Ye h, I heard that the two of you were a thing."

"A thing? What does that mean?"

"You know. A thing."

23

Joe goes through the motions of a school day waiting for it to end. Mulling over questions he wants to ask while on his way to where cheer-leading practice is being held. Before opening the gym doors he sees the captain of the basketball team, down the hall talking with a girl. He can't tell who the girl is because her back is toward him, but they seem to be arguing. This is probably the one he kissed before the big game and they are having a lovers spat. Ah, to be young again and go through the trauma of a teenager's life.

Upon entering the gym, he is struck with the beauty of Miss. Harrison, the coach. He has seen her practically every day in her classroom but here and in a powder blue top and white shorts, she looks entirely different; more sexy.

"Miss Harrison, or should I call you Coach Harrison?"

"Coach Bobby! You can call me anything you want. What brings you to our practice? Do you want to try out?"

"No, if I shook my…pom-poms, it would clear the stands. I'm looking for Amy."

Coach Harrison laughs. "Amy?"

"Amy Singleton."

She looks over the group of girls, each in a different stance. Her eyes pause on a brunette in a mid-air jump.

Motioning for the girl to come forward she calls, "Amy, front and center."

The bubbly wide-eyed Amy darts through the jumble of teenage bodies to stand in front of coach Harrison.

"Coach Bobby wants to talk to you."

Amy turns to Joe.

"Yeah coach?"

All of the other students look down on Joe when talking to him in his wheelchair, but Amy's height puts her at eye level with him.

"I want to ask you about Samantha Parrish."

"What about her?"

"Let's go somewhere where we can talk."

Joe wheels his chair around and heads for the bleachers with Amy strolling beside him.

"Are the two of you friends?"

"Yeah, I guess."

"You guess? You don't know?"

Amy goes two steps up into the bleachers and sits down.

"Sometimes it's hard to tell with Sam. One day we are joking and laughing and the next day she hardly speaks to me. It's as if she is to different people."

"Do you think something is bothering her?"

"Yes, there has to be something, because this isn't like Sam."

"Do you know what it is? Why she is acting like this?"

"I've asked her but she won't tell me. When I try to talk to her about it, it just makes her angry and she gets very obnoxious."

"She gets obnoxious, does she?"

Amy nods her head.

"Last week she called me a meddlesome munchkin."

Joe suppresses a chuckle. "That *is* bad."

"I know."

"Do you know anything about a friend of hers called Chris□ie?"

"I knew her. I didn't know her, I knew of her. I wasn't in their circle of friends. I didn't become Sam's friend until after Chris□ie left."

"Did Sam tell you?"

"No, Sam refuses talk about her, but it was the talk of the school."

"What did you hear?"

"That she was a witch and she cast some kind of evil spell that backfired on her."

"What does that mean?"

"Some spells are so powerful that if the witch isn't strong enough the spell will not only curse the one it is intended for, but it will curse the witch as well."

"You think Chris☐ie accidentally cursed herself?"

"Yes, I do."

"What kind of curse do you think it was?"

Amy leans closer to Joe and whispers.

"I think she changed herself into some kind of animal, like a cat or a bird."

Joe hesitates, not knowing what to say.

"Do you think she is a cat now?"

Amy's eyes enlarge as she gazes into Joe's.

"Yes."

"Now, instead of her parents having a daughter they have a cat?"

Amy nods. "That's why they moved."

Joe leans back in his chair.

"Hum. Do you know where they moved?"

Amy sits up straight smoothing her blouse.

"I think it was New York or someplace like that. I don't know."

"Thank you, Amy you've been a lot of help."

Amy steps off the bleachers on to the gym floor.

"You're welcome coach."

Before she leaves Amy looks intently into Joe's eyes.

"Some people believe that Chris□ie hexed Sam into becoming her friend, but I don't. Sam is the kind of person that will make friends with anyone. I'm sorry we aren't talking right now, but I'm not mad at her. Will you tell her that I will always be her friend, and when she's ready to be mine again let me know?"

"Yes, I'll tell her that. Thank you for talking to me."

Amy half skips, half trots back to the others.

Joe contemplates what the young girl has told him. He wonders if Sam believes her friend is a witch, and what it has to do with her present actions.

24

Gertie is weeding out her flower garden when her cell phone rings. The snapdragons are doing well, but the marigolds need help. She removes her gardening gloves and starts digging into her pocket. By the time she finds her phone the music stops. Clicking the missed calls button, she sees it was Coach Bobby. She hits redial and sits back on her gardening stool. The phone on the other end rings one time before being picked up.

"Hello Gertie?"

"I'm sorry, I couldn't get to the phone in time. I hope you are calling to say you're coming for dinner."

"Uh, no I'm not. I don't mean I'm not coming to diner, I mean that's not why I'm calling. I do want to come to dinner and I intended to call for that, but this isn't it. I was going to call later about dinner, but something came up and I need to talk to you NOW."

Gertrude smiles as she absentmindedly picks at the mulch in front of her.

"What came up that you need so desperately to talk about?"

"Can I come over?"

"Yes, of course. When,"

"I'm halfway there now."

Gertrude leaps to her feet and removes her straw hat as she heads for the house.

"OK! You mean right, now don't you?"

Before he can answer she turns her phone off, races into the house as she drops her hat and gloves in the mud room, and kicks off her muddy shoes. Damn! There isn't enough time to get ready. She needs to get in the tub with her new lavender scented bath salts; that isn't going to happen. She removes her clothes as she races through the house to her bedroom.

A bar of scented Dove soap lay in the soap dish on her bathroom sink that has never been used because it is there for decoration. She runs it over her face and upper body.

THE MULLIGAN

A little deodorant and a couple sprays of perfume will have to suffice. Glancing at the clock as she re-enters her bedroom she begins to panic. What is she going to wear? Picking out a turquoise dress she holds it in front of her as she gazes into the full-length mirror mounted on the back of her closet door. This is her favorite, the short hem line and low-cut neckline is quite seductive. Since Bobby can't wait to see her, this should substantially raise more than his heart rate. As much as she would love to do that, this dress is for evening and it is early afternoon.

Tossing it on the bed her eyes sweep over her extensive wardrobe. She selects and discards five tops before choosing a simple white blouse. A pair of tan slacks completes the ensemble. Casual!

Better not rush things, let him make the move. Now her hair, but before she can do anything about it the doorbell rings. Lightly running a brush over it to smooth any shoots that may be sticking up she hurries to open the door.

The man in her doorway is not what she expected. Instead of a love hungry animal she finds a distraught man.

"Bobby, what's wrong?"

"May I come in?"

Gertie stands aside.

"Of course."

Joe wheels over the threshold, past Gertie, and into the living room.

"It's Sam."

The words no parent wants to hear, but it is the sound of his voice that strikes fear into her. Slamming the door as soon as the wheels of his chair clears, she rushes in front of him. Frantically she searches his face.

"What happened to Sam? Was she in an accident? Is she all right? Bobby tell me what happened to Sam."

"No, no she's fine. I don't mean fine, but there was no accident."

"Something's wrong, what is it?"

"Remember I told you I thought Sam had a secret boyfriend?"

"Yes."

Joe takes hold of Gertie's hand.

"It wasn't a boyfriend. It was a girlfriend."

"I thought… what are you saying? Sam is---?"

"NO! No of course not. Do you remember a friend of hers by the name of Chris□ie?"

"Yes, she was a weird child, but Sam liked her. She and her family moved away, what, a year or so ago?"

"I think Sam's secret has something to do with her."

"The girl had problems but I don't think they involved Sam."

"I think they did. Whatever Chrisie's problem was I think Sam tried to help her, and maybe she couldn't."

"She's been gone for a long time. I don't think Sam has had any contact with her since she left, so why would this come out now?"

"I don't know, but we have to find out."

Out of the corner of his eye Joe notices something behind Gertie, when he looks Haig is standing there.

"Joe your daughter needs you."

"Where is she?"

Gertie shakes her head.

"I don't know."

"Haig, tell me where she is. I need to go to her."

"She's not far from here, in a gazebo in the backyard of her friend Chrisie's old house."

"Is she hurt? Is she all right?"

Gertie looks around the room, there is no one else in sight.

"Who are you talking to Bobby?"

Joe grabs Gert's hand and pulls her with him as he heads for the door.

"Do you know where Chrisie's old house is?"

"On Ralston, why?"

"We have to get over there; that's where Sam is."

"How do you know that?"

"I got a message from heaven."

Joe sees the puzzled look on Gertie's face.
"Don't ask."

25

Gertie closes the door after Joe wheels through and stops. A thought hits him. Will Haig's illusion of him driving, work on Gertie if she is in the van with him? There is no way he can actually drive. He should have insisted that Haig teach him. He has to tell Gertie she has to drive, but then there will be a lot of time wasted while he gets himself and his chair into her car.

Haig whispers into his ear.

"Go in the van Joe, have faith."

Flying down the walk Joe calls back.

"I'll drive."

Haig is right about having faith, because as soon as Joe is behind the wheel, he knows what to do. The gearshift lever is on the right side of the steering wheel along with the brake lever.

A lever on the left feeds gas into the engine. All the controls can be operated with his hands. Joe pulls slowly away from the curb. He pulls on the gas lever and the van picks up speed but they're going to slow; he has to get to is daughter. A hard pull on the gas and the van shoots forward pulling the automobile to the left. Just before they run off of the road and hit a large tree Joe turns the steering wheel to the right, but he over compensates and they bounce back in the other direction. Joe jerks the wheel to the left, but again this is too hard and they head for the other curb. This time he is careful and does not turn the wheel too far and steers straight down the street, with a few wobbles.

Now they are going too fast, Joe panics. He hits the breaking lever and the van comes to a screeching stop throwing both passengers forward. Gertie rubs her shoulder where the seat belt pressed against her.

"Are you all right? What happened?"

Rubbing his chest, Joe smiles.

"I'm all right, but I think I was in too much of a hurry."

"Maybe I should drive."

"No, that's okay. I've got this."

Once more Joe pulls slowly forward. Gertie shouts directions as Joe fumbles with the levers and steering wheel. Ralston is only a few blocks away, but it feels like they have gone several miles when Gertie frantically yells.

"Stop! Pullover. There it is. That's Chrisie's house on the right."

Joe pulls to the curb without hitting it, and stops in front of a two-story older ranch style house. He looks the house over as he waits for the van door to open, and the chairlift to start moving. The house is empty, and it appears to have been so for quite a while. The grass needs mowing and the sidewalk has deteriorated to a sad state. Agonizing seconds that seem like hours click by as the lift descends, allowing Joe to roll onto the curb.

Joe's eyes sweep the yard.

"Where is the gazebo?"

Gertie answers as she grips the handles on Joe's chair.

"Back. The gazebo is in the backyard."

They hurry as quickly as the chair will allow through tall grass and dirt. As they go around the house toward the gazebo and their daughter, the right wheel of the chair hits a stub of a plant that has been cut close to the ground.

Gertie backs the chair up and tries to circumnavigate the obstruction in their path but hits it again. After several attempts she manages to bypass this barrier only to encounter other obstacles in their way. It takes several forward and backward moves to sidestep the obstructions.

Sam is sitting in the corner watching through teary eyes as her Aunt Gertie and Coach Bobby come into view at the corner. They appear to be having difficulty pushing through the grass, even with Joe helping. They slowly bounce over a rolling turf; finally, Gertie leaves Joe to travel the last couple of yards on his own, and falls to the floor beside Sam taking the sobbing girl into her arms.

"Are you okay honey?"

Samantha doesn't speak or move.

Gertie strokes her niece's hair as she consoles the weeping girl.

"Sam, talk to me baby. What is the problem?"

Sam doesn't answer and Gertie continues stroking her hair while tears form in her eyes. She gently leans over and kisses the top of Sam's head.

"Whatever it is honey, or however bad it is, I'm here for you."

Joe manages to get to Sam and Gertie with the help of Haig, but sits at the door unable to get up the high step. His daughter is a few feet in front of him sitting on the floor crying and he can't do anything. He wants desperately to get out of his chair, drag himself across the gazebo floor, and yell at the top of his lungs," Sam I am your father and I'm here to help," and then have her fling herself into his arms. Before he can act on the impulse, he feels a hand on his shoulder.

THE MULLIGAN

Without looking up he knows who it is. The touch has a calming effect on Joe, so he sits back watching the two women. The love between them is overwhelming.

"This is what you came back to see Joe. It appears as if the two of them will be just fine."

Tears seep out of Joe's eyes and run down to fall freely from his chin onto his lap as he watches the scene in front of him. Samantha is in good hands. Gertie has done a fantastic job of raising his daughter so far, and he is sure she will continue. As much as he hates to admit it he knows his daughter will get along fine without him.

"Yes, I know they will and I know I have to leave, but I don't want to go back yet. Can I stay just a little longer?"

"You agreed to return after you were sure Samantha was going to be all right, but technically you have a few hours left. I might get in trouble for this, but we can stay a little longer."

"Thanks Haig, now get me closer to my daughter."

The heavenly guide picks Joe and his chair up and sits him down on the gazebo floor. Joe rolls over to where the women sit. Cupping his daughter's chin in his hand he lifts her head to look into her eyes. The pain he sees there is overwhelming. It is tearing him apart seeing Samantha like this. He has to do something, but he does not know what.

"Samantha pumpkin, we are here to help. Tell us what is bothering you. No matter what it is we will fix it."

Samantha smiles.

"My daddy called me pumpkin when I was small. Before mommy died."

Gertie moves around to sit in front of Sam.

"Honey, talk to us. Please"

Samantha stands and walks to the other side of the gazebo, away from Gertie and Joe.

Keeping her back to them she wipes tears from her eyes.

Joe reaches down and helps Gertie stand. Placing his elbows on the arms of his chair, he folds his hands and places them in his lap, he leans forward. Gertie remembers Joe would lean forward like that when he was trying to make a point.

"Sam, your aunt Gertie and I can help, if you let us. Does Chris□ie have anything to do with this?"

Samantha is stunned by those words. How does he know about Chris□ie? Do they know what happened? Does aunt Gert know what a horrible person her niece is? Sam hesitates, and then she turns to face him.

"I killed her."

Gertie is Shocked.

"WHAT?"

"It was my fault. It was all my fault that she died."

"Honey I'm sure that's not true."

THE MULLIGAN

Gertie starts to go to Sam to comfort her grieving niece, but Joe puts his hand on Gertie's arm stopping her.

"Tell us what happened Sam."

Samantha's head is down and she is playing with a tissue.

"Chris☐ie was a witch, or at least she thought she was. Kids in school taunted her. They thought she was weird because she dressed funny and wanted to be alone, so they teased her and made jokes about her. She tried to stay away from everybody but they wouldn't leave her alone.

"She finally had enough and blew up. She turned on this one girl that had been on her back for a week. I don't remember the girls name, but Chris☐ie mumbled something and waved her arms. The next day the girls face broke out with acne and everyone said that Chris☐ie hexed her."

Joe asked, "did she?"

"Chris☐ie along with everyone else thought she did, but I don't believe it. The girl had been eating chocolate. Anyway, Chris☐ie was ecstatic. She already thought she could cast spells and now this proved she could. She started getting serious about witchcraft. She spent hours at the library and on Google. She bought a black cat to use as a familiar and started burning candles and incense. She studied incantations and drawing pentagrams. I tried to talk her out of this crazy idea but she wouldn't listen. This went on for several weeks, finally I gave up.

I thought, what could happen? She can't really hurt anyone, and it made her happy. I decided to play along. We both lit candles, burned incense, and drew pentagrams.

Angela White was one of the girls that constantly tormented her, so we cast a spell to make Angela fall in love with Donnie Baker."

Joe gives Gertie a questioning look.

"Angela White was the class president, president of the debate society, and president of several other clubs. Donnie was a hoodlum, voted to be the most likely to go to prison. They both graduated before you came to Jefferson."

Joe turned back to his daughter.

"Did it work?"

Gertie shouted, "BOBBY!"

Samantha shook her head.

"No, not right away, but several years after that, they graduated and Angela and Donnie did get married. It didn't last long, but they were married for a while."

Joe gave Gertie a 'I told you' look, and then pressed on.

"At the time though you thought it didn't."

"That's right, we didn't. That didn't stop us from casting more spells though. We cast spells to make noses big, and feet bigger."

"SAMANTHA!"

Sam goes on, ignoring her aunt.

"We gave Ms. Taylor a big butt, but then it wasn't small to start with."

Joe and Gertie wait while Sam paces.

"We were having a good time. Chris□ie was finally a person. Everyone knew who she was. She was 'that witch girl'. They still avoided her, but no one teased her anymore. I even enjoyed it. I was having fun. I still didn't believe in witchcraft, but I played along. One evening when I was at her house the doorbell rang. Her dad opened it and there was a black cauldron and a broom on the porch. Her dad ran down the street, but couldn't find anyone.

"Several months went by and then one day Chris□ie found a dead black cat on her doorstep. There was a note around the cat's neck. It read, 'You are next witch.' This freaked both her parents and us out.

"Why didn't they call the police?"

"They did, but the cops couldn't do anything. No one saw who put the cat there. After that I avoided Chris□ie. We didn't talk and I sat at a different table during lunch. I was scared. I thought they might think I was a witch too, and come after me."

Gertie tries to hold Sam's hand. "Why didn't you tell me about it?"

Sam pulls away.

"In the beginning it was a game; it was fun, but it wasn't a game anymore it was scary. I wanted to tell you about it, but Chris□ie begged me not to. She was too scared and didn't want anyone to find out what happened. She thought if it got out more people might do more horrible things.

A couple of days later Chrisie's father woke up to find a doll of a witch hanging from his tree on fire. A week later her family moved. I found out later that their house was also broken into. Nothing was taken, but the door was left open. It was meant as a message, and it worked because that's when they moved."

Joe speaks lovingly to his beautiful daughter.

"Did you hear from her again?"

Samantha nods her head yes.

"A few weeks after she moved, I got an e-mail from her. Her mother had family in Pennsylvania so that is where they moved. I apologized to her for letting her down; she said she knew I was scared. After that we e-mailed at least once a week. Things seemed to be better for her. She talked about her new school. She made several new friends, both girls and boys.

She fit in there; she wasn't the witch girl. In fact she never mentioned witchcraft. I thought that fantasy was over; it was for me. Last week she told me more about her friends. They were all in her coven."

Surprised Gertie asks, "A witch's coven?"

"I was so angry. I told her how stupid that was. I told her that it was all a game with me; I never did believe in witches. I said some really mean things. I told her that if she insisted on being a witch then never to talk to me again. Yesterday I opened my e-mail and there was one from Chris□ie's' mother. Chris□ie killed herself."

Gertie takes Sam in her arms.

"Oh honey, I'm so sorry."

Samantha hangs onto her aunt and cries.

Joe's heart is breaking. He wants so much to grab his daughter and hug all of the hurt out, but he sits and watches. Samantha pushes away from her aunt.

"If I hadn't been so mean to her, or maybe if I hadn't told her it was just a game for me."

"Maybe if. Maybe, maybe, maybe." Joe is getting angry. "There's always a maybe. You can't blame yourself for what someone else does, or what might have been."

Samantha isn't listening. She starts to pace in circles around the perimeter of the gazebo, while twisting her Kleenex.

Joe and Gertrude both want to do something, but neither know what they can do. Samantha becomes more agitated, turning, and pacing.

She runs out of the gazebo and across the yard. She doesn't know where she is going, she just knows she has to get away from the pain in her heart. She reaches the edge of the yard as Joe and Gertie watch helplessly. She enters the street and stops to catch her breath.

"SAMANTHA, SAMANTHA!"

The words ring in her ears, but she doesn't understand them. It's as if they are coming from a long way off. She wants to run and run until all her feelings are numb.

Joe and Gertie watch Sam run into the street and stop. She puts her hands on her knees in order to breathe better. Terror jumps up and slaps them in the face when they realize a truck is bearing down on Sam.

Joe is yelling at the top of his lungs.

"Samantha Look out, there's a truck coming."

Sam can't hear him.

The truck is getting closer.

Panic sweeps through Joe on the back of a feeling of frustration. His little girl is going to be hurt and he is in this damned wheelchair. Joe's head jerks from side to side frantically searching for… he doesn't know what.

The truck is still coming fast.

People are on the street but no one is paying attention to the two people hysterically shouting and waving their arms.

"HELP! Somebody help!"

Everyone ignores Joe's plea.

The truck is almost on top of Sam now.

Headlights cast an eerie glow on the young girl standing in the middle of the street, as the truck bounces over chuck-holes.

Sam, still bent over slowly raises her head and looks up at the oncoming disaster.

As her eyes register what is happening, realization turns into paralyzing fear.

Joe, still screaming for help, pushes down hard on the wheels of his chair. He reaches the edge of the gazebo's floor but before he tumbles off onto the grass, Walter sets him gently down on the lawn. Without slowing, he races for the street. Tilting from side to side as the wheels fly off the curb one at a time; he rushes on. Struggling to keep his chair upright Joe speeds toward his daughter.

The truck is coming.

Sam is frozen with fear.

Joe is racing to her.

People turn to see what all of the commotion is about.

The truck is almost on top of Sam.

Everything goes into slow motion.

As Joe races toward his daughter he stretches his hands out in front of him. He is moving at a high rate of speed when his hands land on Sam's butt. He shoves with all of his might and with the help of the velocity of the chair, Sam flies across the street onto the grassy berm.

The collision stops Joe's progression, but not the trucks.
Everything goes black.

26

Joe opens his eyes and looks around. He is lying down in the middle of nothing. There is no ceiling or floor, sky or ground. It's as if he is in a room painted all white except there are no walls; no furniture.

SWOOSH!

Joe stands and walks toward the golfer.

"Hey! What happened? There was a truck. Sam was about to be hit. Is she all right? Why am I back here?"

Haig answers without looking up.

"Sam wasn't hit by the truck, and your time is up."

"NO! It can't be. I've got to go back."

"Sorry Joe, you can't."

"Please Haig, talk to someone. Sam needs me. I have to be there for her. I have to help her."

Haig gazes into Joe's face, and speaks with the compassion of a father talking to his son.

"You already have helped her. You prevented her from being hit by a truck, but the truck hit you."

"Are you sure Sam is all right?"

Walter nods his head.

"She's fine now."

"What happened?"

"The truck driver was applying his brakes, so when he hit you, he was barely moving. You were killed, I mean the coach wasn't killed he suffered several injuries, but you were brought back."

"You're sure Sam is all right?"

"When the coach was injured Gertrude was devastated. After several weeks in the hospital, she insisted he move in with her so she could take care him. She stopped eating and socializing, devoting all of her energy to helping the man she loved. Her company began to go down because she wasn't there to take care of it. Sam realized what was happening but she had her own troubles. She was still racked with guilt. When things almost hit bottom, it was Sam that picked herself and her aunt up and the two of them crawled out the whole they were in.

"While Sam was helping her aunt nurse Coach Bobby, he talked to her. He told her that she could not be responsible for another person's actions, and this was a perfect place for a Mulligan."

"But how does he know about a Mulligan?"

"He still retains some of your memories."

"Does he know we switched places?"

"Uh… No." Walter answers emphatically. "He does have some of your memories of her before you died, but he thinks he heard Sam and Gertie talking and they are not his memories.

"Now back to the story, before I was interrupted. Sam finally understood that Christie made the decision to end her own life, and it wasn't her fault. She listened to Coach Bobby and decided to take the mulligan and offer one to her aunt. She talked Gertie into letting her take over all of the nursing duties with the coach so she could get back to her company. Gertie was reluctant at first, but with both Bobby and Sam talking to her she relented and let Samantha take charge. Returning to work wasn't easy, in essence she had to start over. She spent a lot of long nights working, but it paid off.

"Sam and coach got to know each other while spending so much time together. A father daughter love developed. She became the daughter he didn't get a chance to have with his wife, and he became the father Sam needed after losing hers. Now the coach's health is back to where it was, and the size of Gertie's company has doubled. Sam is graduating from college."

Joe's guilt raises its ugly head again.

"I should have been there but I wasn't. It was the same as it has been her whole life. First my career was more important. Then when Connie --- I shut her out because I was feeling sorry for myself. This was my chance to make things right, and I failed."

"You didn't fail. You did what any father would have done, you sacrificed yourself for your daughter. How can you call that failure? Things happened as it was written."

"What? You mean all of that was planned? Everything that happened was intended to happen? I was supposed to go back and fall in love with Gertie and when I was starting to get my daughter back and have a normal life, I was expected to die again?"

"No! It was written that you would change their lives, but not how. What happened between you and Gertrude was your choice."

What happened between you and Sam was also your choice. When you saw your daughter was in danger you acted to save her, that also was your choice. You could have sat there and not done anything blaming your wheelchair for your inadequacies, but you didn't. That is free will, and the actions of a selfless father. We are given the opportunity, and the free will to accept or decline everything that happens in our life."

"Can you at least tell me if they are happy?"

THE MULLIGAN

"I can do better than that."

Haig waves his arms in an arc. A scene comes up in front of them, much like a large TV. In the center stand Sam and Gertie. Both are laughing. Sam is wearing a pastel blue dress, and Gertie a wedding gown. They both turn and a man in a black tux and wheelchair roll in and hugs them. Joe steps back and smiles.

"It was also written that you would borrow coaches' body but that he would reclaim it when you left."

The scene fades and Haig puts his arm around Joe's shoulder and leads him off.

"So, I won't be able to watch my little girl grow up?"

Walter whispers into Joe's ear. Joe smiles and finds himself standing between Gertie and Samantha.

He kisses Gertie on the cheek, and she instantly raises her hand to touch the spot.

"I was wrong about you. You are a beautiful person, both inside and out. You are both kind and loving and I was too blind to see it. This is the Gertrude that Connie knew, the one I wish I could have known. I wish I could spend the rest of your life with you, but I am told that is not what is written. You have done a wonderful job of reshaping your life, and Sam's. No one could have done any better at taking such good care of my little girl. Not many men get the chance to love two fantastic women, but I did. You will be happy with Bobby; he is a good man. I know him pretty well."

153

He takes her hand in his and gently rubs his thumb over her knuckles. She lets out a small gasp as she covers the place with her other hand. A small tear slips out of the corner of her eye making a wet streak down her cheek to fall to the ground.

Leaning in close to Sam he gives her a kiss also.

"I love you Samantha. You have grown into a strong, intelligent, and beautiful woman, but you will always be my little girl. I wish I could have been there while you were growing up, but I couldn't have done any better than your Aunt Gertie. I know now that I don't need to worry about you, every thing is going to be just fine."

I am sure the man you choose to share your life with will be the right one. But just in case I will check up on you now and then and I'll be around if you ever need me. Have a wonderful life pumpkin."

Joe wraps his arms around his daughter squeezing tightly. Reluctantly, he releases her and kisses her on the forehead.

Tears come to Sam's eyes as she glances toward Heaven.

"Daddy is here."

"Yes, I know."

A feeling engulfs Joe that is euphoric. All worries and fears are swept away as he finds himself back with Haig who places his hand on Joe's shoulder and they walk away into the whiteness.

"You can look in on them any time you like, but right now Connie is waiting to see you. She has been acting like a school girl ever since she heard you were coming."

"I want to see her too, but it has been a long time. I hope she isn't disappointed when she sees me."

"I'm sure that will not be a problem. I'll take you to her, but later you have to let me teach you how to play golf. It is a great way to relax and you need to relax.

"Is Heaven like what I've seen so far?"

"You ain't seen nothin' yet. That was the way station for all new arrivals. Now, back to more important things. First of all, you need to learn how to hold a golf club. Take it in your left hand, are you right or left-handed?"

"Right."

"By the way, Sam is dating a promising young man. He's studying law and will graduate with honors this spring. Okay, now take the club in your left hand and ---"

This is not the end, but the beginning.

AFTERWORD

Thank you for reading THE MULLIGAN. I hope you enjoyed it and it delivered all you expected.

Want more information about my future books? Both WP (work in progress), and in the planning stage?

Friend me on: facebook.com/eddielayebookauthor

Join my book club: elaywriter4ebook@gmail.com

AND IF YOU HAVE A MOMENT, PLEASE LEAVE A REVIEW WHERE YOU BOUGHT IT AND MY FB PAGE. THANK YOU.

So, until we meet again between the pages of a book, "Live long, and prosper."

Eddie Lay

THE MULLIGAN

A bit of true facts

Walter Hagen was a professional golfer in the 1920's, wining four Opens, two US Opens, and five US PGA Championships. This got him inducted into the World Golf Hall of Fame. Known for his flamboyant life style by the way he dressed as well the way he spent his money.

While his peers wore shades of gray, Walter dressed in colorful plus fours and two toned shoes. He has been quoted as saying that he didn't want to be a millionaire he just wanted to live like one, and he was the first to make and spend a million dollars.

After Bobby Jones was beat by Walter in a World Championship 72 hole match, he stated: "When a man misses his drive, and then misses his second shot, and then wins the hole with a birdie, it gets my goat."

157

Walter played mind games on his opponents much like boxing champion Muhammad Ali, by calling on them to watch him sink a difficult shot and then declaring to beat them the same way.

The situations his caricature describes in the book actually happened.

Walter was instrumental in changing the attitude toward professional golfers world wide by standing up to the system.

THE MULLIGAN

About the author

I married my wife Sandy in 1966. We have three children, Michelle-Jill-Mark, 9 grandchildren, Jeremy, Brittany, Mark, Samantha, Dalton, Hannah, Christopher, Abbey, Jacob, and one great-grandson, Everett.

At the age of 19, while serving as a combat cinematographer in the US Army, I wrote my first short story. It was titled "A Slight Case of Fear," and I sent it to Alfred Hitchcock who returned it with my first, of many, rejection. After the service I started working at Ford Motor Company, owned a professional photography studio in the Georgetown Shopping Center in Indianapolis, and wrote a weekly column for our local newspaper; The Moorseville-Decater Times. All at the same time.

Realizing I had taken on too much I gave up my writing, and 20 years later in 1988 gave up photography. In 1999, after 35 years, I retired from Ford and returned to writing.

159

Being one of two writers for a weekly children's video titled KidzCan was a great time in my life, and in 2006 I saw my Mystery of the Hats story published in paper back.

OTHER PUBLICATIONS BY EDDIE LAY

WHY DO HUMMINGBIRDS HUM?

A digital book on how to entice hummingbirds to your yard. Released in 2011 this guide is intended to help in attracting hummingbirds, and keeping them.

Available only as an eBook

HANNAH'S HATS

Hannah's Hats was published in paper back in 2006 under the title "Mystery of the Hats".

EDDIE LAY

After finding a strange hat in her closet, Hannah, her best friend Amber, and a neighbor Mrs. Kimble search for the owner of the hat. What they find is murder, deception, and the girl in the white dress.

Available in digital form, but soon to be re-released in print.

MOSSES' DON'T FLY

A children's picture book about Mortimer Moose who wants to fly with Santa on Christmas Eve. He gets his chance when one of the reindeer injures a foot, and auditions are held to replace him. Mortimer goes to the try-outs but is stopped because the rules state that "Only reindeer need apply."

Santa comes to his rescue and opens it to all who live at the North Pole, but in order to win he has to overcome prejudice and bullying. With help from his friends Mortimer succeeds.

Available only as an eBook.

THE KILLING OF SARA LOVE

Big Daddy Brown, a lineman for the Denver Broncos, visits his ill father who talks Big Daddy into replacing him as sheriff until he can return; it will only be a week, or two at most. Everything is fine until a romance novelist is murdered, and bodies start popping-up.

The football playing sheriff realizes that he is over his head, and is ready to give up. Then he is shot at, and his high school sweetheart is threatened. Anger kicks-in and Sheriff Big Daddy Brown vows to bring the culprit to justice, or kill him.

Available in eBook and print.

PRINCESS ABBA DOODLE AND THE WICKED WIZARD

A children's picture book about a princess who, along with several friends, challenge a powerful wizard. In order to return her friend Oscar's voice that was stolen by the wizard, she and her friends have use a magic spell. It will take bravery and faith in herself to defeat him.

Available only in print.

EDDIE LAY

If interested in any of my books; contact me:

www.elaywriter4ebook@gmail.com